A SCOT FOR BETHAN

WELSH REBELS

VIRGINIE MARCONATO

Prologue

Arms wrapped tight around her middle, Bethan stared at the altar in front of her without seeing anything.

Last month she had come to England, and Sheridan Manor, with Jane and a retinue of men. The previous day, after a series of horrific events, her friend had gotten married in this very chapel to the man of her dreams. The bride and groom had met in unusual circumstances and fallen in love, despite Jane being a lady and Griffin a simple villager many considered beneath her. In other words, their story was the exact opposite of what would happen to her.

Her own marriage had been arranged by her father behind her back, an all-too-common occurrence, and it was as far from a love match as could be conceived. She and Dougal Campbell had never met or even exchanged a single letter. And, as future laird of a powerful clan, he would be the one marrying beneath him when he allied himself with the poor daughter of a dispossessed landowner. Would he make her feel unworthy of him once they were husband and wife? She dearly hoped not.

"What are you doing here all alone, Beth?" William, Matthew Hunter's squire, and her friend, spoke from behind her. How long had he been standing in the shadows, watching her fight tears? "Are you all right?"

No, she was not all right. She did not know if she would ever be, considering what fate had in store for her.

"My father has finally found me a husband, the son of an old friend whose life he once saved," she told him in a dull voice. For two years, he had tried to find a match for her, but the suitors he'd approached in the hope of starting to rebuild the family prestige, ambitious men themselves, didn't want a bride without money or connections. She was beautiful enough that they would gladly have taken her to their bed, but a more honorable arrangement was out of the question. "I am to marry a man I don't know. A Scot."

Which meant she would have to leave her home. Not that she had a home to speak of, of course. She was spending most of her time with the Hunters, who were not related to her by blood. Still, to become Dougal's wife, Bethan would have to leave her native Wales.

"Marry? When?"

William sounded as shocked as she felt. But the wedding would not happen for another three years, as she was only fourteen and her future husband, thirteen. It was something, she supposed. Maybe by the time Dougal came to get her, they would have exchanged letters and gotten to know one another a little. Love, of course, was too fanciful a notion to even entertain. This was to be a marriage of convenience, nothing more.

"When I reach my seventeenth birthday."

Another silence. Then a hand landed on her shoulder, warm and comforting. "I'm sorry. I wish there was another way."

"I know. So do I."

But there was no other way. Fate had decided she would marry a Scot, and that was all there was to it.

Chapter One

Wales, spring 1317—Seven years later

Bethan stared at the letter in her hand, its enormous seal as shiny and red as a blood stain.

"A letter from Scotland," the messenger had said as he'd handed her the piece of parchment covered with flowery script.

Scotland. It could mean only one thing. At long last, her betrothed was coming to get her. After more than seven years of waiting and endless delays, Dougal Campbell had finally decided to honor his promise to his dead father and marry her.

On the chair opposite her, Gwenllian was biting her bottom lip. Evidently, her friend had guessed what the missive might be. "Is this it then?" she breathed.

Bethan let out a mirthless laugh. Upon being told about the union her father had arranged for her all those years ago, she had exclaimed that she hoped Dougal would not come until she was an old maid.

Well, she had been made to regret her bitter words ten times over. But it seemed that the wait was about to end.

"Yes, this is it," she answered through gritted teeth. "Dougal is coming."

Or...was he?

Suddenly she wasn't so sure. She and her best friend had often jested that the Scot would end up changing his mind and break off their engagement now that both their fathers, who had arranged the match between them, were dead. After all, he didn't seem interested in marrying her any more than she was in marrying him. It seemed entirely plausible that he should release her from the contract considering his lack of enthusiasm for matrimony. Hadn't he prolonged their three-year betrothal by another four years so he could join Robert the Bruce's army? Didn't he prefer to fight for the independence of his country and besiege castles rather than do his duty by her? Hadn't he ignored the numerous letters she had sent over the years?

Yes, a thousand times, yes.

So, was she holding the key to her freedom in her hand? Had he written to announce she could start finding herself a husband she actually wanted because she was no longer beholden to him? The missive in her hand certainly looked nothing like the two short, perfunctory notes he had sent her before he'd joined the Bruce's men aged barely sixteen. Oh, if only...

Before she allowed hope to bloom in her chest, Bethan broke the seal with a shaky finger and started to read. It was not long before disappointment settled over her shoulders like a lead mantle. This was not the key to her freedom, but rather to the cage she was about to be locked in.

"Dougal has decided it was time we wed but he will not be coming to get me himself. Laird Campbell, his uncle, will be the one escorting me to Scotland. It is easier that way, apparently, as the man speaks English." Her voice took on a dull quality as she carried on. In his two brief missives, her betrothed had made no secret of his refusal to learn the language of his enemies, even if it was the only way the two of them would be able to communicate, at least at first. "We are to be married the day after I arrive. The retinue intends to set off as soon as the snow has melted and should reach Castell Esgyrn at the end of the month. It has all been decided."

The two women stared at one another for a long moment. Not only had her elusive betrothed not changed his mind, but he'd not thought it necessary to come in person to get her. Instead, he'd sent someone else to escort her to her new home. This was a blow, undeniably—*another* blow, she should perhaps say. She had always imagined she and Dougal would have time to get to know one another during the lengthy ride to the Scottish Highlands, in other words, before they became husband and wife. It seemed that she was to be denied even this small boon.

Bethan stilled, resignation seeping to her very core. Deep down she knew the news she'd just received should rouse a reaction out of her, but she just felt numb. Soon she would have to say goodbye to all she knew, settle in an unknown place and, the following day, marry a perfect stranger. It was an appalling prospect, whichever way she looked at it, but she had endured so many setbacks over the years, swallowed so many disillusions that she could not muster the energy to be devastated.

Gwenllian put on a brave smile, determined not to let her own dismay show. "Well, I suppose we knew this day would come."

Yes, they had, which was ironic because none of the rest had gone the way it was supposed to go in that grim affair. When her father had betrothed her to Dougal seven years ago, he had done so on the understanding that her future husband would, in time, succeed his father and become laird. But at the Scot's death a few months ago, the title had gone to Cameron Campbell, Dougal's uncle instead. The clan, understandably, had preferred to elect an experienced man to rule over them rather than take a chance on an untried youth of barely twenty summers who was never there.

In spite of this new development, the arrangement between them had been maintained, for which Bethan was grateful. No one had wanted to ally themselves with the fourteen-year-old granddaughter of a brewer, whose penniless father had been dispossessed of what little he had managed to build by the English King after the conquest. She was now one and twenty, not old exactly, even if it often felt that way, but she was certainly no child bride anymore. And she was still as poor as she had been seven years ago. All in all, she was hardly an enviable party and Dougal's offer was the best she could aspire to.

Bethan sighed. What would her father think of all this? He had arranged her eventual marriage to the prospective Laird Campbell to restore their family's prestige. When he'd died two years after signing the wedding contract, he had gone to his grave comforted in the knowledge that he had made an advantageous match for her. But instead of being the wife of a clan chief, and the lady of the castle, as he had planned, she would end up being married to one of the laird's nephews, a man who was only interested in fighting for his country's independence and likely to be killed before too long as a result.

She looked around, seeing the bedchamber she shared with Gwenllian with new eyes. Soon she would leave Castell Esgyrn, never to return. Though it was not, strictly speaking, her home, it was the place she felt most comfortable in. Because of her friendship with Gwenllian, the Hunter family had always considered her like a daughter. After the death of her father, they had offered to welcome her under their roof. It had been natural to accept their kindness.

In leaving them, she would leave the people she loved the most in this world, the only people who cared for her, except for her brother Siaspar, who had been sent to foster in a castle beyond the valley as a young lad.

Yes, the people of Castell Esgyrn were her family. And yet, close as they were, they didn't know her secret.

The respectable, *betrothed*, Bethan ferch Morgan, was no virgin.

How would Dougal react when he found out? Would he even notice? He was younger than her, so maybe he was not so experienced that he would know the difference. Would he care if he did notice? She was not even sure. Theirs was not a love match, far from it, so he might well not worry about his wife's past, as long as she did not make a fool of him once they were married. The thought that her indiscretion might never be exposed should have reassured her, but it didn't, because it only served to show the lack of interest her future husband took in her. Prolonging their betrothal beyond what was acceptable was proof enough that he had no interest in her. Sending another man to get her on the pretext that he didn't speak English was such a feeble excuse... He could easily have come along and brought an interpreter with him. But no. He didn't care about her, and she doubted that would change when he met her.

As for her... What did she think?

Though she was determined to give this marriage a try, Bethan didn't see how she would ever get on with a man who had not bothered writing to her more than twice in seven years, whose only interest seemed to be in political machinations and whose ways would be utterly foreign to her, at least at first. If he didn't speak English—Welsh had never even been mentioned—then how were they to converse, and get to know one another? She had been unable to find a single person able to teach her Gaelic, so she would have to learn when she reached Scotland. It would take time. An interpreter was all well and good, but having someone constantly lurking in the background, repeating your every word, hardly helped build intimacy. And how would it work when they were alone, in bed? Unable to communicate their doubts and preferences, they would be reduced to copulating like beasts without exchanging a single loving word or voicing out a tender reassurance.

This was one of the reasons she had taken the shocking decision to bed someone before meeting the husband who had been selected for her. She had not wanted her first time to be with a man who would be unable to speak to her during their first joining, comfort her if need be, stop if she begged him. She had also, given Dougal's apparent lack of enthusiasm for this union, started to fear that he would never come to her. The prospect of ending up as an old maid, of dying a virgin and never having known what it was to lie in a man's arms was not a cheerful one. Last of all, and rather foolishly, she had hoped that their engagement would be broken at the death of the old laird, leaving her free to marry a man of her choosing, one who would love her and wouldn't mind her not being untouched.

It had not been difficult to find a lover.

Men had taken an interest in her from a very young age, competing for her favors, choosing to forget she was not free to indulge her senses, boasting about their skill in bed in order to be the one having the honor of making a woman out of her. It had pleased her to ignore those overconfident rogues and give her maidenhead to a shy youth instead. Edward had been perfect, both tender and too awed by her not to do his best to give her the pleasure she was after. In truth, she had intended for William, her friend from Sheridan Manor, to be the first man to possess her, but things had not gone the way she had hoped. When she had tried to kiss him, he had confided the reason why he would never be able to do what she was asking.

That night the whole castle had been celebrating in his

honor. The faithful squire, who had arrived at Sheridan Manor as a page, had finally been made a knight.

Just before the banquet the two friends had gone for a stroll around the bailey, eager for some fresh air after the suffocating heat of the day. Bethan had led him to the herb garden, and a little alcove hidden in the wall. Earlier that day, she taken the precaution of heaping cushions over the stone bench so as to provide maximum comfort. It was the perfect place to put her plan to execution, cozy and private. In the fading light, no one would see them unless they were standing right over them.

Raising herself onto her tiptoes, she placed her lips on William's mouth.

"W-what are you doing, Beth?" he asked, holding her at arm's length, his shock evident.

This was not the reaction she had expected but she did not let it worry her. Bethan knew he would understand when she explained what this was about. He knew about her pending union to Dougal, so he would not judge her. He lived in England, thereby ensuring that this encounter would remain a secret, and he was one of the most caring and handsome men she knew. He would be gentle and mindful of her pleasure.

Yes, William was perfect for what she had in mind.

"What do you think I'm doing?" she breathed, nestling herself against his chest. He felt so good, so tall and broad, hard and deliciously masculine, the perfect foil to her feminine soft-ness. Would Dougal feel as good? She still didn't know anything about his physical appearance. She pushed the uncomfortable thought away. There would soon come a time when she would know exactly how he looked—dressed *and* naked. "Will you show me what pleasure men can give women?"

"I can't." Gently, he pushed her away.

"You need not fear you are taking liberties," she reassured him, aware she was asking a lot from him. Not only was she suggesting he deflowered a virgin, but also a woman who was betrothed to another man. For someone as honorable as he was, such a thing would be unthinkable. But her mind was made up. "I want this, I want to know what it is to be touched by a man I know and trust, someone I chose for myself, before I become—"

"I'm sorry, but as much as I sympathize with your predicament, and would love to help you, I really can't show you what men and women do together."

With those words, William did the last thing she'd expected him to do. He took her hand and placed it between his legs. There was no hardness there, nothing that betrayed any lust. He was not lying. He did not feel any desire for her, which meant he would not be able to possess her, no matter how much she tried to entice him. Everything within her collapsed. How cruel that William should be the only man she had not been able to ensnare with her much-praised beauty. Bethan had lost count of the number of men who had stolen kisses from her and ground their hard members against her stomach in their bid to show her how much they wanted her and how ready they were to make her theirs.

And now, when for the first time she would actually welcome this proof of desire, she felt only soft, unresponsive flesh.

"I see." Never had she felt more dejected.

"No, you don't. This has nothing to do with you." He sounded agonized and he drew her back into a brotherly embrace. "But you see, I, myself, am still waiting to find out how wonderful it is to be touched by a man I trust," he whispered in her ear.

A *man*.

Bethan stilled. Well. If that were the case, then she understood why William could not bed her, why this was indeed not personal. All bitterness forgotten, she melted into the embrace and felt him relax when he saw she did not resent him for his refusal or condemn him for his preferences.

"I understand. And your secret is safe with me."

It was better that way, she had assured herself, as she watched William being congratulated on his achievement later on that evening. He was a dear friend, the only male friend she had, and she didn't want to do anything to compromise their friendship. Besides, it was him who had introduced her to Edward, his cousin, the following day. The handsome groom had been an excellent choice and the two of them had spent a delightful few days teaching one another the pleasure that could be had between lovers.

Since that fateful night, she had become more competent at choosing men who wanted her, and furthering her knowledge of her own and her lovers' bodies. Since she was no longer a virgin, there was no point in denying herself what little excitement she could have for now, she'd reasoned. All too soon, her life would change. Once she was married, only one man would be allowed to touch her. It was the way of the world, so she might as well make her peace with the notion. And who knows, perhaps Dougal, as disappointing a betrothed as he had been, would prove to be a caring husband and skilled lover.

Yes. And perhaps trees in Scotland grew fruits of gold.

Bethan turned to Gwenllian, tears in her eyes. "Yes. It would seem that my time has finally run out."

Damn and blast. The way was blocked.

A quick glance around the courtyard confirmed Bethan's suspicion. While she'd been talking to Mistress Elen upstairs, a group of riders had stopped by the tavern, making a discreet retreat to her horse impossible. One of the men was leaning against the gate leading to the stables. She would never get past him unnoticed. Three others were standing in front of the fire, warming their hands and laughing. They would see her as soon as she stepped out of the door. The only ones who might not notice her were the two relieving themselves in a dark corner, shouting lewd comments and egging each other on as they did. Heat invaded her cheeks when she saw that their arms were moving with frantic, rhythmic gestures and their backs were arched. Were they actually—

A cry of male satisfaction pierced the night, answering her question. They were indeed relieving themselves, but not in the way she'd thought at first.

"Feeling better, Murdo?" one of the men by the fire shouted.

"Aye," he growled back. "Though with my hands so callused, I'd rather have ploughed a woman's sweet—"

Not wishing to hear the rest of the sentence, Bethan clapped her hands over her ears and debated what to do.

She could not step out of the tavern in front of half a dozen men desperate for release. The risk of being mistaken for one of Mistress Elen's girls was too great. But she couldn't stand here all night either, she had to get to her horse and leave without delay. It was late already, much later than she would have liked. Any moment now customers would start to arrive. Getting away would be even more difficult than it was now. Perhaps the element of surprise would play in her favor? It was worth a try.

Avoiding the light shed by the fire burning in the center of the courtyard, Bethan started to walk to the gate on silent feet. A whispered entreaty to the man leaning on it might be enough to make him move out of the way. He might, just might, understand the predicament she was in and let her pass.

By keeping in the shadows and hugging the walls she almost reached the other side of the courtyard before the men spotted her. Once they did, however, their reaction was immediate.

"Whoa there, halt!"

All attempts at discretion forgotten, Bethan started to run to the gate, hoping that the man stationed in front of it would take pity on her and move out of the way in time for her to slip through it.

He did not, even if he made no move to seize her.

With her only escape route blocked, she had no other choice but to halt. Panicked, she watched as two of the men walked toward her on unsteady legs.

"Just where do you think you're going, sweetheart?"

"What's the hurry? Stay a while, we're in need of company."

Bethan's heart sank. These were not only men, but drunken men—and English. The fact had not registered earlier, when she'd heard Murdo and his friend, but they had not spoken in Welsh. Damn and blast indeed! Now she was in serious trouble. A pack of Englishmen could only mean danger to a lone Welsh-woman, especially if they thought she was the kind who earned her living on her back.

Fortunately, living with the Hunter family, she had a reasonable knowledge of the language, even if she spoke it with a much stronger accent than she would have liked, so she would be able to at least try to defend herself.

"I'm not what you think I am," she said before they could get the wrong idea. "I'm a...a l-lady," she stammered.

Well, she wasn't, not exactly, but neither was she a simple villager, much less a whore. And she was *not* going to service them, whatever they thought.

Laughter answered her, as could have been predicted.

"A lady are you now?" the man called Murdo scoffed, joining his two friends. She was relieved to see he had tucked himself back in his braies at least. "We all know that ladies spend their time wandering around taverns at night looking for men. I've lost count of the number of grand noblewomen I've fucked on wooden tables, amidst pitchers of ale. There was even a princess once, if I recall."

"Aye, wasn't she the one who sucked you dry in front of everyone?"

"Nay, that was the Duchess of the Holy Land. Get your story straight, Hamish!"

More laughter. Bethan had no idea how to get out of this. As she had taken care to dirty her face and dress as plainly as she always did when visiting Mistress Elen, she knew that it was ridiculous to claim to be a lady. The disguise usually protected her identity, but it might prove to be her downfall today. She didn't want to give her name, as the last thing she needed was for Lord Sheridan to find out that the girl he was kindly housing under his roof was visiting stewhouses at night to obtain herbs preventing conception. Besides, there was no guarantee the men would believe her if she claimed to be under the protection of the local lord. They seemed too aroused and drunk to see sense.

A shiver of dread slithered down her spine. That she was no virgin didn't mean she wanted to be raped by...how many men were here exactly? At least six. Dear God. She might not survive the ordeal.

"Come, lass, you can see we're harmless men in search of well-earned relief. You have nothing to fear from us. We'll even let you have first pick," another man offered, whilst she debated what to do. He was younger than Murdo, and his speech was less gruff. Still, she was far from reassured. "Who do you want to go first?"

"No one. I just want to get to my horse. Please. I need to go."

She turned back to face the man blocking the way, hoping that he would let her pass this time. All throughout the exchange with his friends he hadn't said a word or budged an inch. In the light of the torch one of the men was holding she saw that he was fixing her intently, his demeanor serious rather than lecherous. It was clear that he was in charge of the retinue, and he was the only one without a drink in his hand.

Bethan stilled, taking him in.

Despite the danger, she found herself thinking that she had never met a man quite like him, so intense and, well, so *stunning*. His eyes in particular stole her breath away. In the light of the flickering flames, they appeared almost transparent, and she couldn't quite decide if they were blue, green, or gray. Not that it mattered, not when they glittered like precious gems.

The rest of him was just as striking. His hair was of a color rarely seen, a deep, fiery auburn too intense to be called ginger and too bright to be merely brown. It glowed in the torch light, but she guessed it would dazzle in the sunshine. The hint of stubble on his square jaw, slightly darker than the hair on his head, gave him an air of virile strength. It wasn't the only thing that did, though. The nose perched above a sensual mouth, the arms crossed over a muscular chest, everything about him exuded power and manly confidence.

As if that were not enough to make him one of the most handsome men she had ever seen, the smile playing on his lips, along with the gleam in his eye, hinted at a sensuality that made something inside her stir. At any other time, she would have felt compelled to try and speak to him. Right now, however, she only wanted to escape the unwanted attention of the drunken men.

Could she dare hope he would see reason? The other men did not believe she was not one Mistress Elen's girls, but Bethan had the odd impression that he wasn't fooled by her humble appearance. It was as if he could see straight to the pretense and to the heart of who she was. His direct stare reached all the way down to the bottom of her soul. No one had ever looked at her with such unnerving intensity before and she couldn't decide if she liked it or not. At least he looked more sensible than the others. It was all that mattered because he was her only hope. If his friends were convinced she was there for their entertainment, she would never make it out of here unscathed. With half a dozen drunken men waiting to take their pleasure with her, she would be lost if the man couldn't help her.

Bethan looked at him beseechingly and opened her mouth—only for her tongue to refuse to move. *Go drapia*, but he really was gorgeous. Or rather, impossibly forbidding. Or...something.

"Please, let me pass," she said after what felt like an eternity. "I just want to get to my horse and ride home. I'm not who you think I am. I truly am a lady."

He let his gaze wander over her as if to decide whether to help her or not. Before he could reach a decision, a man spoke from behind her, his words so slurred she barely understood what he was saying. He had an accent she had never heard before, nothing like the gentle lilt of the Hunters.

"Come on, enough of this, we're waiting here."

A hand shot out from under his cloak, reaching for her shoulder. She tensed, readying herself for the moment he would grab her but before one finger could touch her, the man by the gate captured the roaming hand in what seemed like an iron grip.

"Leave it. She says she's a lady." His voice was deep, and he sounded mightily annoyed at his man's insistence.

"And you believe her? She looks like a tavern wench to me," the lecher protested, trying to extract himself from the hold. In vain. When his commander finally released him, he cradled his wrist with a grimace.

Her defender pursed his lips, eyes alight in amusement. "She does look like a tavern wench," he conceded, eyeing her up and down. "And a particularly dirty one at that. But I'm sure she has a good reason for it. As well as a good explanation for her presence here so late at night."

"I do!" Bethan huffed. Annoyance had started to replace

fear. How long would this farce go on? She needed to get away, now, or the people at Castell Esgyrn would notice her absence and get worried. "Not that I have to share them with you, mind you. Just let me pass."

A raised eyebrow greeted this less than meek answer. "Well, my friends, what say you? Will this show of haughtiness suffice to convince you she is indeed a lady and *not* a girl from the stewhouse?"

Convinced that she had nothing to fear from the man—or his friends now that he had taken her defense—Bethan pressed her suit. "No, I am not a girl from the stewhouse, as I keep telling you. Now if I could just get to my horse."

"Of course. Worry not. My oafish companions will leave you in peace."

He nodded to the men who retreated to the fire without another comment, even the gruff Murdo and the aggressive lecher. Bethan could not help but be impressed by the man's natural authority. At his command the men had gone from rowdy bunch to subdued puppies.

Without a word, she hurried to the stables. Now that the way was finally free, she did not intend to linger any longer than necessary. Heaven only knew what could go wrong next. In the darkness, it took her longer than she would have liked to saddle her mare, and her trembling fingers made the job of putting the bridle on more taxing than usual but eventually, she was ready.

When she emerged from the stables with Petal in tow, the man was still in the same place, watching her. She forced herself not to stare back and instead focused on getting out of here.

"Do you need an escort?" he asked in his deep voice while she led Petal to the mounting block.

"No, I do not."

Bethan hoisted herself into the saddle with decision. The question had made her ill at ease. Had he sent the men away so that he could have her all for himself? If she agreed to have him accompany her, would he waylay her once they were alone in the woods? Did he mean to use her as a reward for his help earlier? She had expected better from him.

He seemed to read her disillusion and smiled.

"You have nothing to fear from me. I did not spare you my men's advances only to force myself on you at the first opportunity." The earnestness in his voice was too obvious for her not to believe him. Her shoulders relaxed. "But how can you be sure you will not meet with other men who mistake you for what you are not and make the same demands on you as my men? As your escort, I could fend them off."

An unbearable heat spread through her body at the thought of him fighting to protect her from ruffians' assault. How arousing it would be... When she moved, she felt the hard nubs of her nipples push against the rough fabric of her shift, something she didn't even know could happen. It caused her to inhale sharply. Not new to the pleasures of the flesh, nevertheless Bethan had never met a man who could make her body melt with a mere glance. Instinct told her that this man whose name she didn't even know would be more accomplished, have more stamina, give her more pleasure than all her other lovers combined.

She shook her head, disgusted at herself. What was wrong with her? Hadn't she come tonight to say her goodbyes to Mistress Elen and the life that had been hers this past year? Before the week was out, she would be on her way to Scotland, and her future husband. She could not be thinking of what it would be like to bed this man, or indeed any man. Once she was Dougal's wife, she intended to be faithful to him. That meant she could not allow handsome strangers' appeal to affect her in any way.

"Don't worry, I'm used to traveling in these parts alone," she answered, desperate to appear more assured than she was feeling. "And I have never yet been forced to go down on my knees to pleasure anyone."

The air seemed to ring with her last words. The man tilted his head, and she blushed furiously. Why, oh why had she said such a thing?

"On your knees. Now, there's an image to leave me with." Bethan swallowed. The low purr would have made her legs waver had she not been sitting in the saddle. "Good night then, *my lady.*"

When she kicked her horse into a trot a moment later, she had the impression she had just been on a reckless ride. She felt out of breath and slightly dizzy.

She was still trembling by the time she reached the safety of her bedchamber. Fortunately, Gwenllian was already asleep, so her escapade would remain a secret. When Bethan started to wash and undress in the velvety darkness, she had the ridiculous impression that she was about to perform the acts the men had wanted her to, but for one of them only.

The man with the sparkling eyes.

Chapter Two

The next morning, the mysterious stranger by the gate was still all Bethan could think about. Try as she may, she just could not get him out of her head. He had made a much stronger impression on her than the few moments they had spent together warranted. It was not just the fact that he had helped her that made it impossible for her to forget him, it was the way he had allowed his gaze to roam over her. She suspected it would haunt her for years to come. It had been sensual rather than lecherous, not marred by any ill-placed possessiveness as was too often the case with men who desired her.

It had been like being stroked when you were used to being groped, a caress and a kiss in lieu of a nip and a bite. Most men just wanted to take their pleasure with her and hoped she got hers in the process, but this man had given her the impression that, for him, giving his lover pleasure was the best way to ensure his.

In her half-awakened state and then in her even wilder dreams, she had pictured the two of them involved in all sorts of scandalous acts. She had been spreading her legs and baring her sex for him to lick. She had dropped to her knees in front of him to pleasure him until he shouted in release, like Murdo had done in the courtyard.

Her cheeks started to burn at the memories, and she was glad to be alone in the bed. Dear God. As she'd pointed out last night, she was *not* a girl from the stewhouse, she shouldn't know about these acts, much less try to imagine what it would feel like to perform them, even with a man of undeniable appeal. Once again, she tried to push these ideas out of her mind. Now certainly wasn't the time to fantasize about strangers.

She was about to meet her betrothed's envoy.

After an agitated night, she had slept later than usual and been awakened by a clatter of hooves on the drawbridge, heralding the arrival of at least half a dozen horses. Though they had not expected the Campbells for another few days, Bethan had instantly guessed the riders would be the ones charged with escorting her back to Scotland. The arrival of the retinue, predictably, had sent the castle into a flurry of activity.

Margie had been at her door within moments, a look of alarm on her face and a heavily embroidered dress in her arms.

"The Scots are asking after you," the old maid told her as soon as she entered.

Yes, they would be. They would be curious to finally see the beauty who had been promised to their laird's nephew.

"You'll have to welcome them alone, I'm afraid," Margie carried on, already fastening the laces on the sides of her bodice with deft gestures. "Lord Sheridan and the family went to the village shortly after dawn. A messenger has been sent to warn them, but it will be a while before they come back."

Bethan could not repress a groan. Could this get any worse? Not only had she been denied what little respite she'd thought to have, but she would have to face dour old Laird Campbell on her own, while her mind was filled with unsuitable images involving a fascinating, fiery-haired stranger.

Still, there was no other choice, so she let herself be trussed up like a fowl ready for the roasting, which was exactly how she felt at the moment. Eventually there was nothing else to do. Everything had been pinned into place, laced, brushed, and smoothed. Knowing she looked as good as she had ever done was small consolation. Considering why they had come, she had no intention of impressing the Scottish delegation.

"Thank you, Margie. I think I'll go down now."

Taking one last deep breath for courage, Bethan descended the spiral staircase. There was no point in delaying the inevitable.

After seven long years of waiting, the second part of her life was about to start. Now was not the time to obsess about a man she would never meet again, or marvel at the unprecedented effect his gaze had had in her body. It was difficult though. Never had she seen a man with such presence and compelling beauty. Now that she was not in front of him, she couldn't help but wonder if she had not imagined it all. It must have been a trick of the light, or rather the absence of adequate lighting that had made him seem so appealing. Either that or she was misremembering him. Surely no one could be that attractive, that sinfully carnal.

No one except...

Except the man standing in the shadow of the keep right now, talking to the castle steward.

Bethan stared in amazement at the man who had come to her aid the previous evening. It was him, there was no doubt about it. Gone were the unkempt stubble and tousled hair, today he was clean shaven, impeccably groomed and wearing a tunic of soft velvet rather than dusty chainmail. Still, she knew it was the same man. Even if her mind had hesitated, her body would have given him away. It reacted as if it had finally been allowed to have what she had been craving for years.

Then a series of thoughts, each more worrying than the last, hit her.

If he was the man who'd been by the gate last night, then the riders waiting in the bailey right now were none others than the ones who had wanted her to pleasure them. And if they were here, it was because they were the Scots charged with escorting her back to Dougal.

Dread shot up her spine. Would they recognize her, expose her to the people of Castell Esgyrn? Maybe not. Today, dressed in all her finery, and with her face clean, she looked nothing like the dirty whore they had thought her to be. Besides, they had no reason to think they could meet such a woman in Lord Sheridan's castle. If she acted as if she had no idea who they were, it would be all right.

After one last nod at the fiery-haired man, the steward walked away. Bethan remained frozen on the last step of the staircase, hidden in the door frame, wondering what to do. Then a man in a black tunic she thought might be Murdo whispered something in the stranger's ear and his response drifted all the way to her.

"McBain is a fool. If he is incapable of managing such a simple task, then I can find plenty of people who can. Make sure to tell him that I'm not above leaving him behind. I've had enough of him."

There it was, the deep voice she remembered. She let its wash over her a moment, before a shiver replaced the warmth created in her body. Dear, oh, dear, he sounded a hundred times more commanding than he had been the evening before, when he had spoken to her, and proportionally intimidating.

This McBain, whoever he was, was in serious trouble.

As was she. If the men who had come to take her to her

husband recognized her, then she would have an awful lot of explaining to do. Her behavior had seemed to amuse the handsome stranger last night, but it could have serious repercussions. If he decided to tell Dougal that his future wife was in the habit of wandering around at night unaccompanied, and had narrowly escaped being used as a whore by a company of inebriated men, her life would become very complicated.

And even if no one recognized her, it wouldn't be much better. She had just spent the night lost in lewd musings involving a man in her betrothed's retinue. Such a thing was not easily forgotten.

Just when she thought of stealing back to her chamber to give herself some time to compose herself, he turned around and saw her standing in the door frame. Their gazes met, and her feet started to move before she could make the decision to go to him.

Once she stopped in front of him, three things became obvious. First of all, his eyes, which had seemed transparent the night before, were actually a silvery shade of gray. Secondly, he was in a foul mood. And finally, most importantly, he hadn't recognized her.

Relief washed through her. Perhaps this would be all right.

"You must be Bethan ferch Morgan," he told her with a bow. The tone was too curt to pass for polite, even if it was obvious that his annoyance was not directed at her but rather at this McBain he'd just described as a fool. It reassured her. He was welcome to be preoccupied if it prevented him from looking too closely at her and seeing that she bore a close resemblance to the woman he'd rescued the night before.

"I am."

"The reports of your beauty were not exaggerated, I see."

How original. Bethan gritted her teeth. She knew she had been accepted by Dougal's father because of her beauty and she had heard her beauty praised too many times not to feel irritated when it was the first thing someone brought up upon meeting her, as if it were the only thing that could be of interest about her. She had expected better from this man. The way he had looked at her by the gate had been more sincere than the bland compliments she had heard a hundred times—and had struck a chord within her. Last night, dirty and disheveled, she had captured his attention. Now that she looked like the lady she would never be, he was acting like every other man she had ever met and saying what he thought she wanted to hear.

"Thank you. I would have hated to disappoint you," she replied somewhat tartly.

The man smiled, clearly intrigued by her reaction, when someone else might have been offended. "I see you like that compliment as much as I like to hear people praise me on my peerless swordsmanship. Such an unimaginative thing to say. I will grant you that I should have done better but, forgive me, I was distracted for a moment."

That was new. Usually no one saw how irritated she was by compliments on her beauty. Or if they did, they didn't comment on it. It was her turn to be intrigued. Perhaps all was not lost. Not that it mattered, of course, since she was to marry Dougal and would never get to make the most of the appeal this man exerted over her.

"The difference is that you earned the right to be praised by honing a difficult skill, and that your expertise is not written on your face for all to see."

"Perhaps not on my face. But I hope it shows on my body."

Oh, it did. Heart drumming in her ears, Bethan did her best to stop her gaze from roving all over his perfect physique. In vain. From such close proximity and in adequate lighting, it was most impressive.

She shuffled her feet, suddenly light-headed. They had to

start talking about something else than her beauty and his impressive body. Like his identity. Why was this man at the head of the retinue? Where was Dougal's grizzled old uncle? It did not surprise her that there had been yet another change of plan, but it was highly unwelcome.

"Why are you here? Was Laird Campbell incapacitated?" she asked, cursing her luck for the unfortunate choice of escort. Couldn't Dougal have sent a less distracting man in lieu of his uncle? Couldn't he have guessed what the sight of such a strong, virile man would do to his bride-to-be? Or was he himself a man of such exceptional appeal that he did not fear comparison?

"Incapacitated?" A spark ignited in the man's eyes. Silver, yes, to match the bronze in his hair, a most unusual combination, as far removed from the sapphire and gold she favored in her lovers as could be. "No. I would argue that I am in full command of my capacities, thank you."

"You mean that *you* are Dougal's uncle?" she exclaimed, too shocked to try and find a more suitable answer. This was Cameron Campbell? She had expected a seasoned soldier a great deal gruffer than the knight looking at her with sparkling eyes. She felt like a sick child might feel after being force-fed honey when they had been bracing themselves for the bitter brew they'd been told would make them feel better.

"I am Dougal's uncle," the man she now knew as Laird Campbell answered, looking at her strangely. "Why? Is there a problem?"

"There isn't. Only I thought you would be..."

Uglier, less strong, less distracting, less...everything.

"Older," she finished in a whisper.

The twitching mouth made it clear he had guessed what she really meant. "Yes. Well, sorry to disappoint but I am not in my dotage yet. I'm only eleven years older than my nephew."

Eleven years. He was thirty-one then, ten years older than

herself, nothing like the decrepit man she had imagined when receiving the letter warning her of Laird Cameron Campbell's arrival.

Just then the steward came back to announce Lord Sheridan had finally arrived and was ready to welcome the Scots.

Laird Campbell gestured at the men to follow. Bethan lowered her face and made sure not to look any of them in the eye. So far, she had not been recognized, and she intended to keep it that way. In the hall, Connor Hunter was waiting for them, standing in front of the dais. Two of his men were stationed at either side of the platform. Bethan was relieved not to be alone with Cameron any longer. Now that she knew who he was, she wished she had never set eyes on the man.

This could all too easily end in disaster.

"My laird, I'm sorry for making you wait but I had gone to the village to see to one of my tenants. We didn't expect you before the end of the week at the very least," Lord Sheridan said, tilting his head in welcome.

"Nay, but the snow melted rather quickly this year and we were able to set off earlier than planned. As my men are a hardened lot, who travel without complaint, we made good time." Cameron Campbell's accent, more rugged than the one she was used to hearing at Castell Esgyrn, charmed her ear. Had he spoken like that the evening before? She couldn't remember. Perhaps now that he had been identified as a Scot, he was not afraid of sounding like one. "We could have arrived yesterday, but after a long ride we did not want to present ourselves in front of the bride-to-be all dusty from the road. We stopped at the nearest tavern. The men wanted to..."

Instead of finishing his sentence, he glanced over to her, a frown on his face. When he stilled, Bethan knew without a doubt that he had recognized her for the woman he had gotten out of his men's clutches. Her heart sank to the pit of her stomach.

"The men thought it best to spend the night there," he finished in a totally different voice.

Bethan's heart rate was now alarmingly high, and she made sure to keep her eyes on Lord Sheridan, wanting to see if he suspected anything was amiss. Fortunately, he did not seem to, even if he had guessed what the delay at the tavern might have been.

"Say no more," Connor said pleasantly.

"Indeed, I dare not. I'm afraid such talk would not be suitable at present."

Cameron's whole demeanor was different now that he had recognized her. Her level of nervousness a hundredfold. She willed herself to behave calmly while the two men discussed the various arrangements involved in getting her to Scotland, but the challenge was proving too hard. Every time her gaze landed on the Scot, her heart seemed to skip a beat.

Or three.

"Shall we give you a moment to get acquainted with your nephew's bride?" Lord Sheridan eventually suggested.

"Thank you, that would be most welcome."

Of course, no one in the room knew that the two of them had already met, after a fashion.

Once they were alone Cameron started to pace around the hall, a hand on the hilt of his sword. Feeling utterly at a loss, Bethan waited for him to speak first. She had the impression that she had just entered a great beast's den and, what was worse, she wasn't sure she didn't want this particular beast to devour her.

"So, we meet again, *my lady*."

His mood had changed again, it was not protective like it had been at the tavern, or irate like earlier in the bailey, or serious like during his discussion with Lord Sheridan but gently mocking, and altogether more worrying. Bethan wished that the earth could swallow her whole.

"We do," she agreed in a low voice.

"It seemed that you lied after all," he carried on, not looking at her. "Because you have no right to the title of lady, have you?"

"Please, could we just forget about last night?" she breathed instead of answering. They both knew she was not nobly born.

At last he ceased his prowling and turned to face her, eyes ablaze. It was then that Bethan realized that forgetting about their previous encounter was never going to happen. He didn't seem prepared to, and she would never forget her reaction to him, or the night she had spent because of it.

"Not easy, I'm afraid." He gave her a smile she imagined to be one of apology, but which did nothing to make her feel more at ease. "Considering your parting words, I am having difficulty not imagining you on your knees in front of me, ready to welcome me between your lips. And you have the perfect mouth for this, which doesn't help, full and sensual."

Bethan gasped. Had he just—Had he dared allude to—

Yes, damn him, he had!

Outrage swept her embarrassment away. "Your men treated me like one of the women in Mistress Elen's employ last night and I despised them for it. It was not the first or even the tenth time I had been harassed by men, but never before have I been mistaken for a whore. You came to my rescue, so I did you the honor of thinking you had more finesse than them. Evidently, I was mistaken. You are just as crude as they are, for all that you now call yourself 'laird.' I may not be a lady, but I am discerning enough to know that you're nothing like Lord Sheridan who, unlike you, was born into the role."

The mocking expression was instantly replaced by one

aimed at making her tremble. It did, even if she tried her best not to show it.

"Have a care," Cameron Campbell said between his teeth. His own temper was about to explode. "You are to marry into my family and become a member of my clan. Do you really think this is the way you should talk to me?"

Oh, she knew she was taking liberties. But so was he.

"I apologize, I should not have mocked you for not being born noble." God knows it was not a taint, she herself had less than prestigious ancestors. "But neither should you have told me you were imagining me on my knees in front of you, ready to offer you relief with my mouth. You are here to escort me to my betrothed, your own nephew. In the circumstances, I am amazed that you should dare to allude to my ability to perform such acts, and on you of all men."

Had she been less irate, Bethan would have been shocked at her brazenness. She never snapped at people, she never contradicted them, even when she was dying to. So where had this unusual courage come from? It was not as if Laird Campbell were harmless, either, quite the contrary. She looked at him warily, fearing that he would make her pay for her impudence. He appeared menacing enough to do it and plenty of men she knew would not hesitate but, to her surprise, he merely laughed.

"Well. Never have I been so thoroughly put in my place. I'm impressed. Though, since you seemed to dislike my comments about your beauty, thinking it lacked originality, you will at least admit that my compliment about your mouth was less conventional."

"Less conventional, yes, I will grant you that," Bethan said in a rasp. Dear God, was he trying to kill her? He had not exactly paid her a compliment, had he? He had called her lips full and sensual, which was not the same at all, and already quite shocking. But he'd then told her he was imagining her on her knees in front of him, and that she had the perfect mouth to suck his cock. Indeed, this was a far cry from what he had told her in the bailey, but did he really imagine she would be pleased? "But not more welcome."

It wasn't, damn it, it was scandalous. Then why was the place between her legs throbbing? Bethan could not make sense of it. She should be outraged, not aroused! But it was as if he'd known that, though she had never dared do such a thing with her lovers, she had secretly fantasized about it. When Mistress Elen's girls had first told her it was something men often requested from them, she had been appalled. But then she had been intrigued. Over the weeks, her curiosity had increased with alarming speed.

And now, she was convinced that, with this man, she would like to try.

Cameron's eyes glittered with such intensity that she wondered if she had not spoken out loud. She made to avert her gaze and found that she could not.

"You're right. I was unforgivably crude. Worry not, it won't happen again, and we will never mention what happened at the tavern to anyone." He paused, the very air between them sizzling. "Or discuss your skill at pleasing men ever again."

"Thank you." The gamble had paid off. Dougal would never hear about her nightly wanderings and ask awkward questions. Relief made her waver on her feet. But perhaps it was too premature because Cameron had not been the only person to see her last night. "Do you think your men can be trusted not to—"

A sharp gesture of the hand interrupted her. "Don't worry about that. You look nothing like you did last night. My men were drunk, they only saw you from behind, and this very briefly. They will never think this finely dressed woman is the dirty girl they mistook for a whore." He tilted his head, seriousness returning. "I confess, however, that now I know who you are, I'm curious as to why you would go wandering alone at night dressed as a commoner."

This was a fair question, Bethan had to admit, even if she would rather he had not asked it. "I had some business with Mistress Elen, who works at the tavern. I thought it safer not to wear my usual clothes to go to her," she said, hoping he would allow her to remain vague. "I was delayed because she was called away just after I'd arrived and I had to wait for her to return. I had not intended to be outside the castle walls after dark."

"No, I imagine you had not." He regarded her more closely. "I can only surmise that this mysterious business of yours was of vital importance. Not only was it irresponsible and unseemly of you to visit a stewhouse, but highly dangerous, as you saw. It could all too easily have ended up badly. I cannot help but wonder if a man was involved."

Oh, he didn't know the half of it. Despite the very private nature of the accusations, accusations she knew she should have denied, she didn't say anything, because he was right. Her business with Mistress Elen had everything to do with her relationship with a man. Or rather, men. She'd had more than one lover in the past year.

An uncomfortable silence settled between them. Bethan knew she should leave. The meeting was over, and Cameron had just made her feel bad about herself. There was nothing to be gained by remaining any longer, except perhaps more humiliation.

"I think it is time for me to get my things ready," she whispered. For a moment, lost in the most disconcerting discussion of her life, she had quite forgotten what was really at stake. "I assume we are to leave for Scotland without delay?"

"We will be ready to leave as soon as you are," he confirmed.

"Very well." Sick to her stomach, she turned to the door. This was it, her last moments at Castell Esgyrn. How was she to bear the departure?

"Wait," Cameron called from behind her. "Before you go, may I at least inquire about last night and ask if you encountered any difficulties after you'd left us?"

Bethan stopped in her tracks. After his barely veiled accusations about having a lover, this concern for her safety took her by surprise. Slowly, she turned to face him again. "No. I made it back to the castle just fine, as you can see."

He nodded. "I can see that you are here. Whether you were assaulted or not on the way is more difficult to ascertain."

He acted as if she was being deliberately evasive and there was genuine concern in his eyes. He really needed the reassurance. Bethan was moved by this proof of solicitude she had not expected. Perhaps the Campbell men were a more understanding breed than their fierce appearance led to suppose. With luck, Dougal would prove just as caring as his uncle. The thought was comforting.

"I... No. I was not bothered in any way," she murmured. "I thank you for asking."

"Good. Now go, I shall see to it that my men are ready to depart as soon as you are."

Chapter Three

When the door closed on Bethan, Cameron took his first real breath since he'd seen her framed in the door at the foot of the keep earlier.

Bloody hell, was he dreaming or had all this really happened?

The whole morning had been a succession of surprises, some more pleasant than others.

The first one had been when a lady in a cream-colored dress had walked up to him with bold, deliberate strides. She had to be the most stunning woman he had ever seen, and he could not understand how that could be. Because if he'd been forced to describe her, nothing in his description would have made her stand out in any way. Her hair was a very common chestnut brown, and her eyes just a shade lighter. Her skin was neither pale nor tanned, and her figure completely average, neither slim nor curvy. And yet... And yet there were auburn streaks dancing in the chestnut tresses, like so many sparks of fire drawing the eye, the brown in her eyes was warm, and sprinkled with surprising green and amber flecks, her skin was smooth and flawless. As to her average figure... The assertive way she moved made it come alive. Her hips swayed in scandalous invitation, her breasts jutted forward, inviting a man's caresses—*his* caresses.

He was still trying to put order to his thoughts when the second, and perhaps most unpleasant surprise of the day, had hit him. This beauty walking to him as if she'd been expecting him all along had to be Bethan ferch Morgan, her nephew's betrothed.

Damn and blast!

How could any man be so cursed as to meet a woman who made his blood heat up and his brain scramble and then be told in the next breath that she was the last person he should take an interest in? What had he done to deserve this? Dougal would be stunned when he met the woman his father had arranged to marry him to all those years ago, the one he had barely spared a thought to in all that time. Even if he was not one to waste time admiring the female form, he would have no choice but to notice her eyes the shape and color of almonds, her wavy hair so lustrous it reminded him of a freshly shelled chestnut, and her red lips ready to be tasted in a slow kiss.

Cameron started.

Why was he looking at Bethan as if she were something to be devoured? Well, perhaps because she *did* look good enough to eat. His groin tightened at the idea of kissing her, then dropping to his knees to find out just how delicious she tasted. He guessed her lips and tongue would be sweet like honey and her soft folds as intoxicating as spiced cream. The impulse to run after her and beg her to open her legs for him shocked and worried him in equal measure. He could not think like that! This woman was about to be wed to his nephew, he should not be fantasizing about things only Dougal would ever be allowed to do to her.

But try as he may, all he could think of was using the table behind him for a purpose that had nothing to do with the one it usually served.

Damn it all, he had promised her only a moment ago not to allude to her skill in bed, and here he was, mouth watering at the idea of licking her into sweet surrender. This was a disaster. Cameron was admittedly a lusty man, his desire had always been easily roused, but this was different, stronger, almost inexplicable. More to the point, she was not a woman he could ever have. Bethan was not free, she was promised to another, and he was charged with escorting her back home. She was the last woman he should think about bedding. He was supposed to protect her body, not use it for his pleasure, and he was meant to guard her maidenhead, not take it himself.

Closing his hand on the hilt of his sword, he stormed out of the hall.

He had to find his men to inform them they would set off again before the day was over. The less time he spent in the temptress' company, the better. He would also warn them they were not to inconvenience Bethan in any way. He had not lied; he doubted they would have recognized her as the woman they had mistaken for a whore the previous evening, but that didn't mean they would not see how exceptionally beautiful she was. They would not act on it, of course, as she was set to marry his nephew, but that might not stop them from treating her in ways that would make her uncomfortable.

He found them at the back of the stables, partaking in a hearty meal with the grooms.

"I have spoken to Lord Sheridan and met Bethan ferch Morgan," he told them, making sure to speak in Gaelic in case they should be overheard. "There is nothing more to do and we will leave before the day is over. Mark my words, I will not tolerate any crudeness in her presence, as she seems quite the shy kind."

This last comment almost wrenched a smile out of him because there was nothing shy in the Welshwoman. The way she had berated him for doing precisely what he was forbidding his men to do was proof enough. But he had to say something to make the men behave.

"Of course, my laird," Murdo said, a smirk curling his lip. "It wouldn't do to shock the little virgin and—"

"No, it most definitely would not," Cameron snapped. "Need I remind you that she is soon to join not only my clan, but also my family? You will treat her with nothing less than the respect she is due."

"Aye," the men said as one.

"Don't mind Murdo, you know how ill-tempered he gets when he is away from home," Angus added, glancing toward his friend, who scowled back, proving the point. "He's like a bear with a sore head. Still, worry not, we'll look after the lady."

"She's not really a lady, as you know, and will never be, married to Dougal."

Cameron started. Why had he felt the need to point that out? It was not like him to be so petty. The reminder, however, did not seem to matter to Angus, who nodded toward the keep meaningfully.

"She lives in this grand castle; she was all but raised by Lord Sheridan. As far as we're concerned, she's a lady, and we'll treat her as such."

Cameron barely repressed a snort, remembering how the previous night the men had refused to believe her claim that she was a lady and how they had wanted to treat her. Well, when they saw her in her finery, they would be shocked into respect, that much was certain. He trusted them unconditionally. They could be rough at times, and they were not above letting their bodily urges overwhelm them on occasion, but they were good men.

All except McBain, that was.

McBain was a fool, but Dougal had insisted that his childhood friend join the retinue sent to fetch his bride. Cameron had often wondered if his nephew had not included the man to act as a spy. But to what end? That was what he could not fathom. Had he feared that his betrothed's rumored beauty would entice the men into behaving like randy beasts? Surely he knew that Cameron would never let anything happen to her? Or was it worse? Did he mistrust him, his own uncle, thinking that he might try to seduce Bethan before they reached Crois Dhubh?

He stiffened his spine, not pleased by the notion, because had she been anyone else, he would most probably have tried to do just that.

"Well, I will not countenance any—"

He was interrupted when Hamish's eyes widened so much, they became in danger of falling off from their sockets. Something in the bailey had caught his attention, it seemed. Or perhaps *someone*. Someone too stunning to be believed in her cream dress. Cameron turned in time to see Bethan draw to a halt in front of him. Though he had seen her only a moment ago, he was struck anew by her beauty. No wonder the men looked as if they had just seen a heavenly apparition.

"My laird, a word with you, if I may," she said in her heavily accented English.

"But of course."

He led her away from the men, glad to see they had indeed not recognized her for the woman they had accosted so crudely the night before. This was one issue he would have to deal with.

"What is it?" he asked once they were a safe distance from the stables.

"I have a favor to ask of you," Behan said, staring him straight in the eye. "I know you want to depart as soon as possible, but I would like to say goodbye to my friends, Gwenllian and Seren, before leaving. They are still at the village with Lady Sheridan, their mother, and I would hate to leave before being able to—"

Her bottom lip started to wobble, and he saw how painful this separation would be. If she had indeed been raised here, then Lord Sheridan's two younger daughters would be like sisters to her. In this moment, he felt like an executioner dragging an innocent victim to the block on the order of some cruel king.

Cameron cleared his throat, waiting for her to get a hold on her emotions. She soon did, which did not surprise him. The woman seemed to have more backbone than most people he knew.

"There's also my brother, Siaspar," she carried on, her voice firm once more. "He lives a day's ride away, to the east. Perhaps we could stop there for the night tomorrow? It would be the perfect opportunity to say goodbye. Not expecting you to arrive for a few days yet, I had planned to visit him before leaving. I would hate to leave without having seen him one last time."

How could he refuse her this second, perfectly reasonable favor? If her brother's castle was to the east, then it made sense to go there anyway. A small detour would be worth the comfort of proper bedding and hot food. There would be enough nights spent on the road during their ride north.

"Very well," he agreed, deciding it cost nothing to grant her this boon. "We will depart on the morrow, once you have said your goodbyes to the Hunters."

A little delay wouldn't hurt. After waiting for seven long years to set eyes on his betrothed, Dougal could wait an extra day, could he not?

It was only when Bethan smiled her thanks that Cameron remembered the reason why he had elected to return home as quickly as possible. He was too susceptible to her charms by far. But how could he not be? He was just a man, and she was a woman of exceptional appeal. Last night he had been impressed by her courage, charmed by her voice and her unusual accent, but he had barely noticed her appearance. In the darkness and under the grime, he had not really seen what she looked like, and the shapeless gown she'd been wearing could have hidden even the most glaring deformities. Now that she was clean and wearing a dress worthy of the name, however, he could see that every inch of her was perfection.

Well, he had better make to keep his urges under control and ensure McBain didn't report to Dougal that his uncle was lusting after his new wife.

Saying goodbye was even harder than Bethan had imagined. It probably didn't help that she had barely slept that night. For long moments she had lain awake next to an equally weepy Gwenllian.

And now the moment had come.

"Say you will visit soon," Seren urged her, her face scrunched up in a grimace.

"If you don't, we'll only come to get you," Gwenllian warned.

Atop her mare, Petal, Bethan could only smile. If she opened her mouth, tried to say anything, the tears she was trying to keep at bay would fall. Besides, what could she say? Everyone knew that once she was in Scotland, the opportunity to see one another would be, if not nonexistent, at least rare enough. There was no use pointing it out.

She glanced at Cameron who, despite his obvious discomfort and eagerness to leave, was giving her the time she needed.

This was a kindness she had not expected. Even his men, mounted on stallions each fiercer than the next, betrayed no impatience. They simply waited for her to signal that she was ready. In the end, it was Lord Sheridan who put an end to the difficult moment.

"Come," he said, wrapping an arm around Gwenllian's shoulders while Esyllt drew Seren to her side. "Let us allow Bethan to leave with our assurances than she will be welcome here or at Sheridan Manor anytime she wants."

He nodded at her, a fatherly gesture, and, unable to bear the warmth in his eyes, Bethan kicked her mount into a canter. It was time to go. A moment later, she was galloping on the east road with the retinue of Scots hot on her heels.

There, Cameron Campbell surprised her yet again. Not only did he not ask her to slow down, but he also shouted to his men that they were not to try and catch her. He seemed to understand she was not trying to escape but needed the wild ride to free herself of the pain crushing her chest. Either that or he was eager to make up for lost time and deliver her to her husband as soon as possible. The thought was what eventually made her slow down. She was certainly in no hurry to reach Dougal.

"Feeling better?" he asked when he finally drew up next to her, his stallion panting as hard as her mare was.

"No." How could she? She was sick at the idea of all she had just lost. A ride, even a reckless one, was hardly going to change that. "But I thank you for giving me the impression, brief as it was, that I was free."

"No one is free," he told her, his tone somber. "We each have our burden to bear."

Yes. And didn't she know it? Her temper flared at the cruel reminder.

"I was bartered off at fourteen and then spent seven long

years waiting for my future groom to remember he was supposed to marry me. I've just been taken away from everyone I love, I'm being escorted to a foreign land so I can marry a man I do not know and who cares nothing for me," she said hotly. What did he have to offer that could start to compare? She doubted this man had ever been made to do anything he didn't want to do. "I'm a woman, I have no choice but to go along with what others have chosen for me."

"Well, I'm a man and the same applies to me. I never wanted to be laird," was his blunt answer. "But I was chosen and, as even I could see that it was the safest option for the clan, I accepted. 'Tis no use bemoaning what cannot be changed, it only leads to discontent."

All the fight went out of Bethan at the words. 'Twas no use indeed. In less than two weeks she would be married, no matter what. She might as well make her peace with it.

The rest of the ride was accomplished mostly in silence, with her giving Cameron the occasional direction to Castell y Ddraig. Fortunately, sensing her despair, he didn't insist on making useless remarks or asking insipid questions. This restraint found favor with her. Most people she knew would have forced her to endure meaningless chatter, thinking it would distract her.

The only notable incident happened after they had stopped to water the horses the second time. As Bethan drew near Cameron while he had his back to her, he started to fire off what she imagined to be instructions in rapid Gaelic. It was obvious he had mistaken her for one of the men and had not meant to make her ill at ease, but being unable to understand any of the words only highlighted all she had lost—and her powerlessness. Was this what her life would be from now on? Would she be forced to listen to people talking and jesting in a foreign tongue and not be able to take part? She would learn, of course, in time, and she was hopeful she would pick it up as easily as she had picked up English but for a few, crucial months she would be at a loss.

"If you think that's pleasant, then let us see how you like me talking to you in Welsh," she retorted in that language, making sure to talk as fast and as loud as she could. He was not the only one who could bark.

Cameron stiffened and turned to face her. Something was swirling in his eyes, but it was not censure, which made her feel rather guilty. Bethan reddened. In truth, she had overreacted, and she would have to ask for his forgiveness. It was clear he had not meant to bark at *her*. He opened his mouth and, instead of the apology she had thought to receive, she received a volley of what sounded like angry curses in the same gruff language as before. Though he hadn't understood her words, he'd guessed it was a rebuke, and he refused to be chastised for what had been a mistake.

Not to be outdone, she tilted her head and carried on Welsh. "Is that all you've got? I think you can do better, my laird. Or are you scared to say what you really want to say because I'm a woman and you think my sensibilities should be preserved? It would be a first, would it not?"

His lips twitched, and a short sentence was uttered next, just as incomprehensible. But it almost sounded as if he'd understood what she'd said and accepted her challenge.

"Yes, I bet you are," she replied, choosing her answer at random. Their little game was starting to have an odd effect on her. She had been angry at first, and she was now... What was she exactly? She didn't know, but the whole thing was strangely soothing. It was as if she could be herself in front of him, with all her faults, and still be appreciated.

"You're a vixen, you know that?" he said, finally switching to English.

"And you're a scoundrel, but I'm sure I'm not the first person to tell you as much," she answered in the same language—and in the same teasing tone. "Admit it, you used your best foul language just then."

"I might have. Alas, you shall never know." This time the corner of his lips lifted. He *was* amused. "You enjoyed that, did you not?"

She had, inexplicable as it was. What satisfaction could she have derived from the exchange? Each had had no idea what the other was saying. It should have been frustrating. And yet there was an undeniable warmth in her chest. "Yes, I did."

"I did too." The gray eyes lit up. "Truce?"

"Truce."

He nodded and led the way back to the horses. "I will make sure to tell the men not to use Gaelic until we reach Crois Dhubh, even between themselves, and I will not either. It will be better for you that way."

"Thank you."

He'd understood the powerlessness she had felt, and he sympathized. This further proof of thoughtfulness touched her. Though he was taking her away from all she knew and loved, he was not the one at fault. His signature was not the one on the wedding contract. The two of them didn't have to be enemies. Feeling better than she had all day, Bethan hoisted herself back in the saddle. A moment later they were riding again.

"This reminds me, what does Crois Dhubh mean?" she asked Cameron, coming to ride side by side with him. She had wondered from the moment she had been told the name of her future home what it could mean, but had found no one who could translate it for her.

"Black cross," he answered in his deep burr.

"Oh." Though the name was not particularly inspiring, she forced herself to be sensible and read nothing into it. Castell

Esgyrn meant Bones Castle and yet it was the most pleasant, welcoming place you could imagine. Perhaps Crois Dhubh would be nowhere near as sinister as the name suggested. Still, she had to admit the image it had conjured up in her mind was rather grim. "And what about your own estate?"

He hesitated, as if reluctant to answer. "It's called Nead an Diabhail. It means 'Devil's Nest,'" he added when she arched a brow.

"I see." Devil, no less. Well. She'd asked, had she not? "Is everything in Scotland so...formidable?"

The word died on her lips when he threw her an amused look. "Aye, I guess most things are. But don't let it impress you. I hear that Castell Esgyrn means Bones Castle. It cannot get more sinister than that, and yet you'll agree that there is nothing remotely fearsome about the place."

She was surprised he was aware of the meaning of the castle's name. He had to have asked for the translation, for how else would he know? The thought warmed her. At least someone in the Campbell family seemed interested in her. "Yes. The workers found two skeletons in the ditch when they dug the foundations to build it a century or so ago, hence the name."

Cameron chuckled, something she would have thought him incapable of. Men like him didn't chuckle. It was not just that he looked like a warrior, dressed in chainmail and atop a mighty charger horse, although it certainly made it odd to see him act as an amused child, but he seemed too...well too formidable to have such a reaction. And undeniably, it was endearing.

"I hope Ned..."

"Nead an Diabhail," he supplied when she faltered.

"Thank you. I hope Nead an Diabhail is not called Devil's Nest for a similar reason."

Another chuckle. Another beat her heart skipped.

"You ken, I've never wondered why it was called like that.

But now that I think of it, I doubt the Devil has ever set foot by the *loch,* much less built a nest there. It's much too peaceful a place, nothing like the fiery pits he favors. You'll soon see for yourself, as 'tis only half a day's ride away from Crois Dhubh, right next to a stream going by the name of Demon's Bowels and a wee rock the local children call the Crooked Tooth."

She recoiled at the list of ominous names. Just where was she headed? "Really?"

This time he winked. "Nay, I'm jesting with you. Not all names are that bad, and I'm sure you'll be just fine."

Bethan didn't answer, as she suddenly felt unsettled. Cameron Campbell could be whimsical. It was quite unexpected, and though she wasn't sure why, it unnerved her. His thoughtfulness had been a pleasant discovery, but she wasn't sure how to deal with this side of him. It was odd because there was nothing she liked more than to exchange pleasantries with people. With him, it seemed dangerous somehow.

By midafternoon, they reached the small but pretty castle that was now Siaspar's home. Her brother had succeeded in doing what their father had tried his whole life to do. Hardworking, clever, and determined, he had earned himself the respect and affection of the ageing lord he'd been sent to foster with at a young age. When the man had died, a few months after his only son had been killed quite stupidly during a hunt, he had left his estate to the only person worthy of the succession in his eyes.

As a result, aged only twenty, Siaspar ap Morgan was master of Castell y Ddraig. It was a stunning achievement for a brewer's grandson, undoubtedly, and Bethan was proud of him. He had not let his father's dispossession affect him and had built a future for himself on his own merit, unlike her, who would owe her subsistence and what little status she'd have to a husband she had not even chosen herself.

Pushing the sobering thought away, she nudged Petal

onward and rode under the portcullis at a brisk trot. Her brother would be expecting her, and she was equally eager to see him. Earlier that day, Hamish had been sent ahead with a message from her to make sure everything was ready when the retinue arrived.

"*Chwaer!*"

Bethan almost dissolved into sobs when Siaspar called her "sister" with such emotion. This might well be the last time she ever heard the familiar endearment—or even saw him. The idea was too awful to contemplate.

While brother and sister fell into one another's arms, Cameron looked around the bailey appreciatively. The place was well-maintained and two men at arms were patrolling the battlements despite the lack of immediate threat. Though he was the same age as Dougal, the Welsh boy was proving a much more efficient administrator than his nephew would ever be. Would that Crois Dhubh was as half as welcoming and well-guarded as this estate... Poor Bethan was in for a rude awakening, if this was what she was expecting.

His gaze went back to her. The affection between her and her brother was obvious. As soon as she had dismounted, she had thrown herself into his arms. The two of them spent a long moment talking together in Welsh under their breaths, while the Scots glanced at one another uneasily. Cameron thought he understood the reason behind the looks. They, like him, felt like executioners about to lead their victim to the block.

When Siaspar ap Morgan finally drew away from the embrace, it was clear from his scowling countenance that he was as opposed to his sister's marriage to a Scot as she herself was. Nevertheless, he addressed him with all marks of civility, thereby proving he was not one to hold unnecessary grudges. He knew this union had been decided by others.

"Welcome to Castell y Ddraig, my lord, or should I say, my

laird." His English was even more accented than Bethan's, which was hardly surprising. He, unlike her, had not been raised at Castell Esgyrn and would have had fewer opportunities to practice. At least they could communicate, which was the important thing.

"I thank you."

Cameron had never been one for seeing beauty in men, but he couldn't help but see it in Bethan's younger brother. With thick chestnut hair and sparkling brown eyes, Siaspar was the masculine version of his sister, which was to say he was a stunning man.

"I do not like the idea of Bethan being sent to Scotland to marry a stranger," the Welshman surprised him by saying next. Clearly, like his brazen sister, he was not one to be intimidated. "It bothered me when the contract was signed all those years ago, and it still bothers me now. Though I tried to find a flaw within it many a time, I could not. Unfortunately, our fathers made sure the contract was unbreakable. Can you at least assure me that she will be well treated?"

Everything bristled within Cameron at the idea of Bethan being mistreated and he glared at the Welshman for even daring to suggest he would let such a thing happen. "She will be. I'll see to it myself."

A twinge of guilt made him frown. Why had he said that? He had made it sound as if *he* would be the one looking after Bethan, night and day, when they all knew he wouldn't even be at Crois Dhubh with her.

"How will you do that?" Siaspar arched a brow. He had not missed his vehemence. "You are not the one who will marry her, are you?"

"No. But she is marrying into my clan and my family. Therefore, her happiness is my responsibility."

"Happiness? Surely you mean safety?"

Damn and blast, the man was far too astute for a twenty-year-old. Cameron clenched his jaw. Siaspar might be a formidable opponent, but that didn't mean he had to allow him to win. Where was the confident man and level-headed laird he prided himself on being?

"My whole existence is dedicated to ensuring no one under my care has reason to be unhappy," he stated firmly. This, at least, was true. The men around him grumbled their agreement, adding weight to his declaration.

For a moment, the two men stared at one another, not backing down. Eventually, the youth nodded. Oddly, though, this victory felt hollow.

"Shall we?" Siaspar offered. "I daresay you will all be thirsty and famished."

They were, so Cameron accepted the invitation to follow him into the great hall while his men were directed to the stables, where food was already being taken. Castell y Ddraig was run efficiently indeed. Did Bethan share her brother's flair for management, he wondered? She had better do, as Dougal would likely spend most of his time away, in the Bruce's army, and Crois Dhubh was in sore need of repairs. She would be the one in charge of putting it to rights.

Not for the first time, he found himself bemoaning his step-brother's decision to marry his son to a woman he didn't know, and who was obviously looking for a real marriage, not just an advantageous match.

Well, it was as Siaspar ap Morgan had said, it could not be helped.

Chapter Four

A rainbow!

Despite her heavy heart, Bethan's chest swelled in delight. Two perfect arcs, one bright and close to the ground, and a bigger, paler one higher up, were stretching their colors over the valley. It was as if nature was intent on cheering her up with this vision of beauty. Saying goodbye to Siaspar earlier that morning had been just as hard as parting from the Hunters had been the day before and she dearly needed this small moment of joy.

"Please, could we stop a moment to admire the rainbow?" she asked Cameron, who was riding just behind her, as was his custom. "I've never seen such vivid colors."

From the way he arched his brow she fully expected him to refuse. He had reiterated his intention to press on when they'd left Castell y Ddraig and she knew he was eager to reach Scotland. The request to stop, and for such a trivial reason, was sure to irritate him.

But to her surprise, he agreed with a gracious tilt of the head. She could even have sworn he was amused. This was unhoped for. Not wanting to give him the opportunity to change his mind, she jumped down from the saddle and walked over to the edge of the cliff. Handing the reins of his stallion to Murdo, Cameron followed her.

"The view is quite breathtaking, don't you think?" she exclaimed, looking at the rich carpet unfurling at her feet. After a brief morning shower, the sun was shining once more, and everything was bursting with color and life. The breeze was making the tall grass in the fields undulate like waves on a rolling sea. "So beautiful."

"Aye, 'tis beautiful."

Bethan kept her back turned because she had a sudden suspicion they weren't talking about quite the same view. Was he admiring the grass dancing in the wind—or her? His voice had gone suspiciously hoarse.

Heat flared in her body because she was suddenly certain he was looking at the swell of her buttocks. Instinct told her that was where his gaze would come to rest. It wasn't the first time she'd noticed how he looked at her, like a man would look at his next conquest, definitely not the way an old uncle would look upon his nephew's intended bride. She had been on the receiving end of such looks too many times not to recognize them. But with Cameron it was different, better. He didn't just give her the impression he found her beautiful. He made her *feel* beautiful. Up until now, she had accepted what people, and men in particular, told her because it seemed silly not to. She was beautiful, it was the general opinion. It was the first time she had felt it, though.

Trying her best to appear relaxed, she took another step forward. Before she could take another, Cameron seized her by the elbow.

"Careful. 'Twould be a rather nasty fall from here."

"Don't worry, I have no intention of falling," she whispered. Did he really think her so clumsy? Or did he fear she would throw herself off the cliff to escape a union she did not want? It was not impossible, but she didn't protest. The heat of his hand on her arm was as wonderful as it was unsettling and prevented her from thinking straight.

"No one ever intends to fall," his tone gruff. "And yet it happens."

Yes. It did. She had not intended to be attracted to the man charged with taking her to her betrothed, but that was exactly what had happened. Bethan took in a shaky breath.

She was falling indeed. Hard.

It had been a lost cause from the start, she had to admit. At the tavern, his solicitude and manly presence had struck her. Once she had seen his face in the sunlight, the attraction had become stronger than was wise. And now that she knew about his penchant for mischief and his protectiveness, she wasn't sure how she could resist the lure of him.

A rainbow. A *bloody* rainbow. Cameron shook his head in disbelief.

What was the woman doing? She was not above talking about servicing men on her knees yet here she was, displaying incomprehensible enthusiasm for an arc of colors thrown haphazardly over the horizon. She'd brought a company of armed men to a halt in order to admire something only a child would get excited about. And the worst of it was, he'd allowed it.

Forget her, what the hell was wrong with *him*? He'd never been so foolishly weak before, especially when he had a mission to accomplish.

"Come," he said, more gruffly than he'd intended, pulling her back from the edge of the cliff. His heart had jumped in his throat when she'd bent over the abyss, and this reaction had fanned his annoyance anew. What was he doing, worrying about her thus? He had better come back to indifference where she was concerned, and fast. But how? It already seemed too late.

Last night at Castell y Ddraig he had been unable to detach his gaze from her. Being with her brother had brought out the best in her. She'd been relaxed, she'd smiled, she'd laughed, she'd been even more beautiful than usual—and he'd been utterly entranced. As if that weren't enough to make him feel bad, in the morning he'd had to be the one to put an end to the moment. Feeling like he was doing something wrong always brought out the worst in him and today was no exception.

"We've wasted enough time already."

Seeing the light die in her eyes when she finally looked at him pierced his heart. *Mo chreach!* Did he really have to be such a bastard? What harm was there in her enjoying a beautiful sight before starting her new life? A life she hadn't chosen and didn't want? None. He was too unsettled in her presence, that was the problem. But it wasn't her fault he found the idea of her being married to Dougal increasingly hard to bear, it wasn't her fault he was battling ill-advised feelings for her. He shouldn't unleash his temper on her.

Bethan walked away from the cliff edge without a word.

"Wait," he called, intent on telling her she could enjoy the rainbow for a little bit longer. After all, it would not be long before it disappeared.

"Why?" The word was as biting as the icicles hanging from tree branches on a winter's day. "As you say, we've wasted enough time already. After seven long years and countless delays, having sent his uncle to escort me, I wager Dougal is eager to meet his bride. I would hate to keep him waiting for a moment longer than necessary."

Thoroughly chastened, Cameron turned around to face the valley.

The sky was clear once more. As if nature had decided there

was no point wasting its best colors if no one was there to appreciate them, the rainbow had vanished into the air.

The day was unseasonably warm. After the downpour earlier, the sun had started to shine with fierce intent. More used to the stark climate of his native land than sunny afternoons, Cameron soon decided to call for another halt. The horse needed a drink, and he needed a break from looking at the lady riding in front of him. All day long he had looked at her straight back, betraying a courage he could not help but admire, at her hips swaying in unison with the horse's movement, betraying a sensuality he could not help but want to explore.

Perhaps he should ride ahead of the company, from now on, or at least by her side. Then he might not be so affected by the arousing sight.

"I was about to ask for a halt myself," McBain replied. "My head is pounding something fierce after the excesses of last night. I'm afraid I overindulged in the excellent ale we were offered."

"Aye. So I noticed," Carmeron said dryly. The man had made a fool of himself, just like that night at the tavern. It was quickly becoming a habit.

Bethan gave a side smile, looking almost glad to hear of McBain's suffering. Apparently, she didn't like the man any better than he did himself. Ah, so she was a good judge of character, also.

"Our grandfather was a brewer, so Siaspar knows a thing or two about good ale," she told the men.

"Indeed, it was delicious. That doesn't mean his guests should ridicule themselves by drinking three times more than they should, though. I suggest a dunk in the river to clear your head," he added, addressing himself to McBain once more.

And if you drowned, that wouldn't be the end of the world.

What a bloody fool. Cameron couldn't wait to arrive and be rid of the man. He would be sent where he belonged, back to his father's cottage on the other side of the *loch* to tend to his sheep. It was all he was good for. No wonder the clan had preferred to ask Cameron to succeed the old laird. That Dougal gave his trust to men like McBain was proof enough of his inability to surround himself with competent advisors. God only knew what would have happened if he'd been put in charge of the clan. His nephew might well be as brave as any soldier on the battlefield, having taken part in sieges and ambushes from a young age, but he lacked the ability to choose trustworthy men to administer his domains. Ah well, he supposed, everyone had their purpose in life. At least the Campbells' loss was the Bruce's gain.

Having spotted the perfect place for watering the horses, Cameron called a halt.

Bethan made her way toward the river as soon as she had jumped from the saddle. Graceful as a water nymph, she knelt down on the gravel beach. Cupping the crystalline liquid into her palm, she drank, closing her eyes as if to better savor the flavor of the water. Cameron's groin tightened. God on the cross, if she made him hard by drinking water from a stream, what could she not achieve if she ever decided to seduce him? Would she ever dare? Of course not, yet it seemed to him that every time their gazes met, the same spark ignited in her as it did in him. Damnation, why did the first woman to provoke his desire in such a shocking manner have to be the one promised to his blasted nephew? For years he'd heard her name mentioned, and not once had he thought that he would lust after her when they finally met.

But lust he most certainly did.

Was it because they had met outside Mistress Elen's house, before he'd known who she was? Because of her unfortunate comment about never having gone down on her knees for a man? Because of her incredible beauty? He had no idea, but he suspected there was more to it than mere physical attraction. If he only wanted to bed her, he would not want to talk to her while they were on horseback, would he? If he only lusted after her, he would not want to tease her about demons' bowels and crooked teeth, would he? That was certainly not his usual method for wooing females.

The scene by the cliff that morning had made him understand that the irritation he felt in her presence was not due to her, but to him and his inability to cope with the desire she stirred in him, and he'd been uncomfortable ever since.

And then, as if he'd needed another reason to be irritated, McBain planted himself in front of him.

"Laird. A word with you, if I may."

The hairs at the back of Cameron's neck instantly prickled. The man had spoken in Gaelic, despite his express instructions that they were to speak only in English during the journey, so as not to make Bethan ill at ease. Nevertheless, as there might be a good reason for the change, and Bethan was down by the river, out of hearing range, he answered in the same language.

"What is it?"

"I spent the last two days wondering where I had seen the Welshwoman's horse before."

Cameron barely repressed a growl. Why was it that he always corrected his men when they called Bethan "my lady," and yet he wanted to snap McBain's neck for calling her "the Welshwoman?" It had to be because he could not stand the man, he decided, *not* because he didn't like to hear her being talked about so casually.

And then the meaning of McBain's words hit him.

He thought he had seen Petal, Bethan's mare, before. And of course he had, that night at the tavern, when the men had thought her a whore. This could prove disastrous. No one at Crois Dhubh could know that Dougal's future wife had been seen in a stewhouse and been propositioned by his men. That was bad enough, but inevitably, the story would become distorted. It wouldn't be long before word got round that she had been seen with her skirts round her ankles and a lover thrusting between her legs.

He turned to the man and said in his most uninterested voice. "Have you? That was a waste of time, if you ask me, because you can't have."

"Well... Maybe I can. You remember the night we stopped at the tavern before we reached Castle Ergwin?"

"Castell Esgyrn, you mean?"

"Aye. That's what I said."

No, it wasn't but Cameron was doing his best to give the impression this conversation was of no interest to him, so he didn't insist. "I vaguely remember, yes." Or rather, he remembered it very vividly.

"Well, that night I saw that horse." He nodded toward Petal, who was munching on some grass next to his stallion. "It was dark, so I didn't see the color of the mare's coat as well as I see it now, admittedly, but I saw her face. No doubt she is named Petal because of the petal-shaped marking on her forehead. It's quite distinctive."

Damn it, the man was a fool, but an observant fool. "You saw a horse with a white mark on its face that night. What of it?"

How long could he keep pretending he had no idea where the man was going with this, Cameron wondered? But betraying no alarm was the safest way to act.

"Not a horse, *that* horse. Don't you see? If the horse was there, it means that Bethan felch Morvan—"

"Ferch Morgan."

"Aye, well if her horse was there, it means that she is the whore who—"

Cameron moved before he knew what he was doing. A heartbeat later McBain was pinned to the nearest tree, his feet dangling a few inches in the air. "If you ever, ever, call the woman who is to marry into my family, my nephew's longtime betrothed, my future niece by marriage, a whore again, you will find yourself without a tongue with which to spread your slander. Are we clear?"

"But—"

"You say you saw a horse with a white marking on its forehead while out of your mind with drink. Well, I say it means nothing. Why should I trust you remember anything of that night? Hundreds of horses sport such markings, and yet you think that's enough to go around accusing a lady of depraved behavior?"

"She's not a lady, she just said herself that her grandfather was a brewer."

Mo chreach! Was the man determined to have his tongue ripped out of his mouth and his bollocks fed to the dogs? It certainly appeared so. Cameron would have liked nothing more than to indulge him, but he could not.

"McBain. If I ever hear you say, or hint, or even think such a thing of the woman again, I will make sure you wish you had kept your foul mouth shut," he hissed, bringing his face inches away from the vile man's. "The horse at the tavern that night, which I saw better than you since *I*, unlike you, was not in my cups, did have a white marking on its forehead. It also was a stallion. Now look again and tell me. Do you see anything dangling between Lady Bethan's mare's legs?" He narrowed his eyes, indicating there was only one way to answer the question.

"N-no."

"Well then, we are agreed it cannot be the same beast. Now make sure you do not tempt me to cut off whatever sorry appendage is dangling between *your* legs. It would not take much to convince me."

"Yes, my laird."

"Good. Now go and plunge yourself in the river. You stink."

He released the man and watched him leave on unsteady legs. Then he took a moment to calm the anger boiling in his veins. Murdo and Hamish, having seen the altercation, arched a brow in question. He shook his head, and they didn't insist, even though it must look obvious that he was in a towering rage.

Bethan was braver, inevitably. A moment later, she approached, a frown on her face. "Is aught amiss?"

"Nay." He probably sounded too curt for her to believe him, but what else could he say?

I almost killed a man for calling you a whore.

Mercifully, she didn't press him.

"Where will we stop for the night?" she asked instead, following him back to the group of horses.

Lord Sheridan had been kind enough to give him letters of recommendation to be handed at the gate of two of the castles situated along the way, on the English side of the boarder. His friends would welcome them on those two nights but other than that, they would have to rely on themselves to find a place to sleep.

"We won't be stopping in a tavern, you'll be pleased to know," he growled. As well as putting him in a fool mood, his conversation with McBain had made him see that someone else's memory might be jolted if they met with women plying their trade. He couldn't risk such a thing happening.

Bethan blushed, and he cursed himself for reminding her of what had happened the night they'd met, when she would have been afraid of what half a dozen drunken men could do to her. "It's not a problem if we have to. I daresay today I do not look like a—well, I don't think anyone would mistake me for what I'm not."

Don't look! Cameron urged himself. *Don't look at the perfect breasts straining under the bodice, at the perfect hips wrapped in velvet, at the perfect mouth putting you in mind of scandalous acts.*

He did look. Of course, he did. He couldn't help it. It would be like asking him not to drink when he was thirsty, not to move when he was drowning, not to smile when he was happy. But at least she was right about one thing. Today she looked every inch the lady.

"Aye. No one would even dare suggest you're anything other than respectable," he growled. "In any case, while I'm with you no harm will befall you, whether on the road or at a place of ill repute."

"This I do not doubt for a moment."

"Is that a compliment?" A corner of his mouth lifted up. How was that even possible? In the mood he was in, nothing should be able to amuse him. And why did he care if she had paid him a compliment? "I'm flattered."

"It's a statement of fact, nothing more. You are here to take me to Scotland and deliver me to my future husband safe and whole. I doubt you will allow anyone to make you fail in your mission. You are far too proud for that, my laird." She arched a brow, and a spark appeared in her eyes, making them lighter than usual. "I imagine that the only people you allow to get the better of you are the lovers you take to your bed."

This scandalous answer surprised a bark of laughter out of

him. How was it that she could coax him out of his foul temper with only a few sentences?

"Indeed. Surrendering to a beautiful woman's will feels like the sweetest victory."

"Has it happened often?"

"Not nearly often enough. In my experience, most women think that it is their role to be passive. They expect men to take them and enjoy every moment of it, but they would never think to—" he stopped, realizing what he was saying. Why was he discussing such things with the maiden promised to his nephew? Hadn't he promised he would never allude to her skill in bed? True he was not talking about her, but he was sure he had crossed the line into unsuitable the moment he'd mentioned the pleasure there was in surrendering to a beautiful woman's will.

By rights, Bethan should lash out at him, but she surprised—or rather shocked—him by finishing his sentence in his stead. "They would never think of riding their lover and give him, as well as themselves, immense pleasure in the process."

For a moment he just stared at her, too stunned to react. What the hell did she know about riding a man? Once he had recovered his wits, he answered. "Such language for a well-bred young maiden! I imagine you got used to hearing bawdy talk at the tavern, but I do hope that plain speaking is the worst thing Mistress Elen's girls taught you. Or perhaps not, since you seem to know an awful lot about what women do to men when on their knees."

She might be still a virgin, and yet not be completely innocent.

This time Bethan's cheeks went a deep crimson. He would have found the color delightful if it hadn't betrayed her guilt. *Did* she have some experience with men then? She'd claimed she had never gone down on her knees to pleasure a lover, but that didn't mean she had not kissed anyone or used her hand to—

"Didn't you agree you would not discuss my skill as a lover?" she said, cutting through the unbearable image of her taking a man in hand to give him blessed relief.

His eyes narrowed. He was not the one at fault here and they both knew it. "You started it, with your talk of women riding their lovers. Besides, it wasn't a personal comment. I said what 'women' do on their knees."

"I'm a woman, am I not?"

Och, aye, she was. Every inch of her was definitely, exquisitely, unmistakably female. A man like Dougal would never be able to handle her. He would panic.

And just like that, his anger deflated.

What sort of life awaited Bethan in Scotland, he wondered for the hundredth time? The more Cameron thought about it, the more worried he got, because he feared she would waste away in the foreign land. At first, not knowing anyone, not being able to converse with the people, she would be lonely, that much was certain, and he didn't see how things would improve afterward. A boy of twenty, spending more time in Robert the Bruce's army than at home getting to know her, his nephew would be a poor husband. He wouldn't know what to do with a wife in his castle and a woman in his bed.

At least... Cameron could be mistaken, but he was pretty certain Dougal was a virgin, with little or no idea how to please a woman. Not only had his mind been occupied by thoughts of war for years, but even as a youth, he had never expressed any interest in any girl. It would be highly surprising if he could offer his bride a satisfactory consummation and fulfilling marital life. He would not even have the will to try, thinking it a woman's duty to lie back and allow her husband to take his pleasure whenever the mood took him or when he thought it was time to get another child on her. Would Bethan try to show him what delights they could share? The women from the stewhouse had clearly taught her a thing or two, even if she claimed never to have put them in practice. Would she want to experiment with her new husband? Dougal was pleasing enough to the eye. She might well wish to—

He brought an abrupt halt to the musings. Imagining the newlyweds in bed together was torture. Dougal didn't deserve such a fine wife as this Welsh beauty. If the boy was to marry someone he didn't love and would only ignore, why couldn't it be a cold, religious fanatic who would be relieved to be spared her husband's attentions in bed?

Bethan was anything but cold and dispassionate. If her attitude in life was any indication, she would be a fiery lover, afraid of nothing. Hadn't she forced a retinue of men to stop so that she could admire a rainbow? Wasn't she brave enough to put him in his place every time he snapped at her and bold enough to ask what he did to his lovers? A woman such as her needed a life companion, someone to bandy words about by day—and a real man in her bed at night. Someone like him, who liked nothing better, as he'd just told her, than to surrender to a brazen woman's will when the time and place were right.

Oh, but what he wouldn't give to surrender to *her* will.

God's teeth, but things were progressing at an alarming pace if he was imagining himself in bed under her, allowing her to use his body for her pleasure. They had only been together for a few days, and had at least another fortnight's travel ahead of them. How would he endure it? Thankfully, at that moment Angus called him, providing the perfect excuse to put an end to the dangerous conversation.

"If you'll excuse me." With a curt nod, he walked away.

Dear, oh, dear, what mess had she gotten herself into?

Left alone, Bethan wavered on her feet. Never once in the

seven years she had spent waiting for her Scottish husband to finally come to her had she imagined that she would meet the man of her dreams in the retinue which would escort her to Crois Dhubh, but she now feared she had. Not one of the men she had taken to her bed in the last few months had made her feel so...alive, for want of a better word. When she had received the letter informing her that Dougal's uncle would be the one escorting her, the last thing she had expected was that she would fall under his spell.

His earlier words came back to her.

No one ever intends to fall. And yet it happens.

Yes, it did. It had. And it was a disaster. What if he told his nephew that his betrothed was lusting after another man, a man who was none other than his uncle?

No, he would never do that. Because she was certain she wasn't the only one to feel the tension between them, which only made everything worse. Had she been anyone else than Dougal's future wife, Cameron would have acted on the desire they felt for one another by now. He would have carried her to the woods and ravished her until she couldn't move. But of course, he couldn't.

Dear God, this was a mess.

"My lady."

Surprised out of her lewd reverie, she turned to find one of the men, the one called Angus, behind her, holding a big leaf piled up high with juicy berries.

"Yes?" she asked warily. She had started to accept that none of the men knew who she was but, as she could not guarantee an ill-placed comment would not give her away, she preferred to keep contact with them to a minimum. That night, at the tavern, Angus had told her she could choose which of the men could go first. What if he suddenly remembered?

"I thought... That is... I saw these and I thought you might like to have something refreshing to eat in this heat."

Bethan stared in incredulity. Was he offering her berries, for no other reason than to see to her comfort? It would seem so. Ridiculously touched, she accepted the leaf he was handing her. "I thank you, I will indeed. But you do know I'm not a lady?"

Angus shrugged. "So I've been told by the laird. But you look like one, and I cannot very well call you 'Bethan,' now, can I?"

No, perhaps not. "Well, thank you...Angus, is it?"

"Aye, Angus. At your service."

After one last bow, he walked away, leaving her to eat the berries alone. They were delicious, both tart and sweet, just what she needed. Once she had finished, she joined the retinue, who was ready to depart.

"Did you ask the men to go pick berries for me?" she asked Cameron, who was tightening his saddle girth.

"Berries? Nay. Why?"

"Angus just presented me with a handful. I thought perhaps you had instructed them to find the fruit." She shook her head. "I'm surprised he would bother to do such a thing."

"Don't be. I told you; they are good men. When they are in their cups and in need of female company, they can be a bit rough, but they would never have forced you into anything that night." He skewered her with a stare. "They only addressed you the way they did because they thought you were there in search of customers, a reasonable assumption given your attire and the fact that you were there at all."

"Yes." Oddly, she believed him. The men could easily have pounced instead of trying to talk her into accepting their advances and they had not needed to be told twice to leave her alone. She saw now that she had been in no real danger. "If that is the case, you could have spared yourself the trouble of coming to my rescue?"

Cameron gave her a side smile. "They would not have taken you against your will, but it would have taken an awful lot of effort on your part to convince them that you didn't want their coin. Remember, they thought you were one of Mistress Elen's girls, and it's what they do."

"Of course. Then, thank you. Indeed I owe you my thanks." He'd not known her, and yet he had not hesitated in helping her.

"'Twas nothing. Now, about tonight. Have you ever slept outside by a fire?"

"No."

"Would you like to?"

"Yes." The word was out before she could think. This would be an adventure, and with half a dozen fierce Scots to guard her, she had nothing to fear.

Cameron's eyes twinkled. "Perfect. Then let's ride. We only have a few hours of daylight left."

Later that night, comfortably settled in a shallow depression dug by Murdo, covered with Hamish's own blanket, which he had insisted be hers to use for the rest of the trip, Bethan reflected on the danger of false first impressions. A few days ago, she would have sworn the group of rough-looking men were nothing but dangerous lechers, a danger to women. She now knew they were nothing of the sort.

Would Dougal be as thoughtful as Angus, who'd gone out of his way to tempt her palate? As efficient as Murdo, who had seen to her comfort before she'd even realized what she needed? As attractive as his uncle, who made her heart beat faster every time she set eyes on him? If he was, then this union might not be such a disaster. For the first time since she'd been told she was going to marry a Scot, Bethan felt some measure of hope.

It was not long before she fell into a deep sleep.

Chapter Five

"Please, my laird, sit."

"I thank you."

Cameron sat down next to Sir Patrick, Bethan to his right. Indeed, a hot meal would be most welcome. For three nights on a row the retinue had slept under the stars, and eaten what food they could purchase in the villages but today the weather had forced them to find refuge in a nearby castle.

Sir Patrick, who owned the place, had been delighted to welcome a retinue of strong-looking men under his roof.

"'Tis my niece's christening the day after tomorrow and we are in sore need of men to keep company to—and most especially dance with—my numerous daughters, sisters, nieces, and cousins. My family has been blessed with a surfeit of beautiful women, you see."

The man, a jovial individual two decades his senior, let out a short laugh. Cameron took an instant liking to him. He was calling the women beautiful, and he'd used the word "blessed" when many others might have said "cursed." Men, as a rule, wanted sons to succeed them, warriors to advance their family's prestige in battles. Cameron, however, had always thought he would like nothing more than being surrounded by sweet-smelling, mischievous daughters. After a lifetime spent dealing with rowdy, somewhat unkempt Campbell men, he was ready for a change.

"A blessing, indeed," he murmured, not wishing to dwell on the thought of himself holding a bairn in his arms one day.

"Yes. The only drawback is that we men are sadly outnumbered at family events," Sir Patrick continued, before letting out another chuckle. "But we need not be today. Your presence here is quite providential. Please say you will stay and attend the banquet on Saturday. A couple of days delay cannot hurt, surely?"

Cameron shook his head in surrender. Seeing as the whole world seemed intent on making a mockery of his resolve to spend as little time as possible with Bethan, he might as well surrender graciously.

"Of course. We'll be delighted to repay your generosity by providing the women company on Saturday," he agreed when Bethan nodded her own assent.

The men, as could have been expected, had been only too happy to comply, and so it had been decided.

This having been settled, Sir Patrick gave his orders to the servants and soon, the smell of freshly cooked bread and meat roasted with spices filled the hall. Aye, their meeting with their host was propitious indeed. The rain could be heard hammering down in the bailey, making it clear they were better off around a table, enjoying a hearty meal, than sleeping outside in the woods.

As Sir Patrick and his wife shared their trencher, Cameron found himself sharing his with Bethan. It was not the first time he'd eaten in proximity to a woman at a feast, of course, but this time it felt disturbingly intimate.

The way she was enjoying her meal stirred something inside

him. She was taking her time, smelling the pottage before bringing the spoon to her lips, eyeing up the slice of suckling pig before taking her first bite. When the taste of the spiced meat hit her tongue, her eyes fluttered. Later, when she bit into her pigeon pie, she groaned in delight. The sound of that groan shot straight to his cock. It was clear that, for her, eating was a deeply sensual experience. If she behaved like this when she was eating, it would definitely be worth finding out what she was like in bed.

Cameron's fingers tightened on his knife handle. He had to stop this, he could *not* entertain such thoughts about his nephew's betrothed, no matter how much she attracted him, no matter how long they were forced to remain in each other's company. Perhaps he should take the opportunity of this halt at the castle to bed a wench or two, cool the blood roaring in his veins in the hope that he would be able to be more sensible afterward. There were a few buxom servants milling about, who seemed delighted by the arrival of a retinue of Scots. Judging from the way they eyed him up, he would not find it hard to find a willing partner while he was here. But, alas, none of the women held any interest for him.

The only one he wanted in his arms was the only one he had no right to, the one sitting so close to him that their knees brushed every time they moved.

The meal soon drew to a close. Cameron let out a sigh of relief and frustration combined as he stood up. His body was tense, but his appetite for food, at least, had been well satisfied. The custard pies, in particular, had been exquisite, cinnamon having been liberally dusted onto the top. This bode well for the banquet to come.

"I would like to go for a stroll if I may, seeing that the rain has finally stopped," Bethan declared, standing up in turn. "We haven't had much opportunity to walk of late."

Indeed, being on horseback all day, they had not been able to stretch their legs. Whenever they stopped, Cameron preferred not to let her wander out of sight and, to her credit, she had not complained. One never knew who or what might lurk in the shadows. But here, within the castle walls, she would be safe, so he nodded his agreement.

Instead of heading for the door, as he had expected, she tilted her head expectantly. "Won't you accompany me, my laird?"

He stared at her in disbelief. It wasn't just the whole world who was conspiring to keep them together, it was Bethan herself. How could he fight if that were the case?

"Aye," he said, before offering his arm. Out of nowhere, his words from a few days ago came back to him.

Surrendering to a beautiful woman's will feels like the sweetest victory.

He'd been talking about bedsport, of course, but that statement could apply to what was happening right now. She was more than beautiful—and he was surrendering to her desire to go for a stroll, unwise as it was.

Bethan took the arm Cameron was offering with a thudding heart. What had possessed her to ask him to accompany her? Couldn't she have gone for a stroll on her own? It would have been the sensible thing to do. But she could not resist stealing a private moment with him because for once they didn't have anything to do other than talk. There were no fires to tend to, no horses to feed, no danger to look out for.

They retrieved their cloaks and exited the hall.

Torches had been placed at regular intervals around the inner bailey, allowing them to get their bearings but as soon as they passed through the gate and entered the outer ward, darkness descended. The thin crescent of moon hanging above the battlements was shedding barely enough light for them to see where they were going. Bethan slowed down, unsure of her footing. Should they turn back? No. With Cameron's solid body by her side, she would not fall.

"What did you want to do with your life, if not become laird?" she asked, once all the light and sound from the great hall had vanished into the night.

She started. Where had that question come from?

"Why would you want to know that?" Cameron apparently agreed that the question was an odd one to ask him.

She shrugged. Though she suspected she was only trying to ensure her mind didn't start to wander down forbidden paths, she could not deny being curious. "We have been riding together for days, and I still don't know anything about you. It feels wrong."

They took a few more steps and she wondered if he was going to answer. Eventually, he stopped and sighed. "Dougal's father, Niall, was only my half-brother, and a lot older than me."

This was not new to her. Her father had once tried to explain the intricacies of the Campbell family to her, but she had barely listened to him, thinking it of little interest. Now she was most certainly interested. "Was he?"

"He was born from our father's first wife, the daughter of the chief of a powerful clan. He was the oldest of three brothers but the other two died at a young age in mysterious circumstances, from what I've been told. I am the old laird's second wife's son, and she died soon after birthing me. I have no memories of her. All I know is that I look a lot like her, and we have the same eyes."

Bethan clenched her fists. Why had she asked him a question that would reawaken the pain of his loss? This was where curiosity led, and she should have known better than to pry. "I'm s-sorry," she stammered.

White teeth gleamed in the darkness, betraying the fact that

Cameron was smiling. Relief made her shoulders sag. Despite her indiscretion, he was not angry with her.

"Don't be sorry. 'Tis all a very grim affair. He had married her only because her father, a local merchant of some importance, had demanded he did so when her belly started to swell with his child—me. The clan elders made it clear they thought my mother was not suited to the role of Lady Campbell, unlike his first wife, and they never saw me as a fit second son for their laird."

"I'm sorry," she repeated.

He smiled again, as if amused that she should ignore his instructions not to be sorry. But she was sorry—and, unlike him, she did not see what could be funny in that story.

"I've made my peace with it. The miracle is that the laird did not ignore the merchant's demand or pretend not to be the bairn's father. Who could have forced him? Nay, though he plainly did not love her and his clan resented him for it, he married the woman and when she died a year later, he vowed never to wed again. Of course, that did not prevent him from fathering half a dozen bastards on local women."

Dear Lord, that was awful, but this time Bethan managed to stop herself from telling him she was sorry. He'd probably guessed it anyway.

"Why did the clan choose you as laird instead of Dougal?"

She was not familiar with succession rights of the Scottish Highlands, but she knew from her father that Niall Campbell had meant for his son to succeed him—it had been the whole reason this union had been arranged, so that she would gain prestige. It seemed odd on the part of the elders to contravene the late laird's wishes, especially when the man they had chosen had not been well-liked as a child. Dougal had been a man at his father's death, not a babe in arms, and by all accounts a brave soldier. He would have been the obvious choice to succeed him. So why had he been rejected?

Cameron crossed his arms over his chest. He really *was* amused, she realized. Perhaps he didn't mind her asking questions, since they seemed to give him such pleasure.

"Unlike Sir Patrick's family, we Campbells are riddled with men." He scoffed. "Not lily-livered courtiers either, but rough, battle-hardened warriors hard to keep under control. Not a sensible woman in sight. When Niall died, the elders felt someone like Dougal, who is not only young but hardly ever home, would never be able to rule over such a rowdy, opinionated bunch. So they chose me, as unsuitable as I was deemed when I was born. I've always had a good head for numbers, and I can be as rowdy and opinionated as the best of them. Apparently, it was enough."

The irony of it. It must have pleased Cameron to take his revenge on the men who had reviled him as a child. But he still hadn't answered her question. What would he have wanted to do rather than keep difficult men under control?

"Why did you accept if you had other plans? As I see it, you didn't owe these men anything. They had despised your mother and made your life a misery. You would have been well justified in sending them to hell."

Instead of being shocked at her choice of words, he shrugged, a gesture that had become familiar over the last week. Odd how you could have the impression that you had known some people all your life. From the moment she had seen Cameron outside that tavern, she had felt a connection to him, as if their meeting was only a question of time. He'd seamlessly become part of the fabric of her life.

"Refusing would have been the selfish option. Too many people depended on me. The tenants have done nothing to hurt me, and they need a strong laird to protect them from our neighbors, who are always looking for excuses to stir trouble. Despite the recent victories of the Bruce, times have never been more uncertain. My clan deserves the best protection, and I am the man to provide it."

Bethan was well and truly chastened. He had sacrificed himself for others, he was doing his duty by people who had treated him badly as a child and protecting others who had never even met him and would never know what he had done. Would she have acted the same in his place? She wasn't sure.

"It was commendable of you," she muttered, feeling inadequate.

"Aye, well that's me. Honorable to the core and putting duty before pleasure."

Though he was obviously jesting to put her at ease, she knew he was telling the absolute truth. He would always put others' needs before his own. Besides, the words were too evocative not to be a provocation, and she reacted accordingly. Pleasure. Yes, if ever there was a man who'd been created to give and receive pleasure, it was him. The hand still in the crook of his arm was resting on rock hard muscle. Was the rest of him as hard, she wondered? Did he—

"And I like to roll around in mud, naked in the moonlight."

"I beg your pardon?" Bethan's head snapped toward Cameron. Had he just said—?

He laughed, the sound uncharacteristically joyous. "It is a relief to see that you *are* listening to me. For a moment it looked as if you were lost in thought and I was talking to myself."

Bethan blushed because she had indeed been lost in the most wanton musings, as was customary in his presence. She could not be next to him without imagining the two of them in bed together, locked in all kinds of scandalous positions, and the mention of him naked did little to help her regain her composure. Yes, he would be hard all over, she suspected, perfect to plunge inside her softness.

"I'm sorry," she mumbled. "I was distracted for a moment. It was most rude of me."

"Worry not, I've survived worse blows," he said roundly. "If you were distracted, I suppose it is my own fault for not making my conversation more interesting. Well, let me set your mind at rest. I do not roll around in mud, naked or otherwise."

Stop talking about being naked! she almost screamed. She was spending far too much time imagining it already and this didn't help.

"I'm glad to hear it."

He scoffed. "Come, it's getting late. Let us make the most of having a comfortable bed for the night."

The air around them stilled. *He doesn't mean it like that,* Bethan told herself. *He doesn't mean he intends to use the bed to swive you senseless in privacy and comfort, only that it should allow you to have a restful night.* More's the pity.

"Yes. I need a good sleep," she managed to whisper.

It had been a miscalculation.

Bethan had thought it best to place herself close to the altar during the mass, knowing that otherwise she would have spent the whole service craning her neck to catch a glimpse of Cameron, but she was now questioning her decision.

Her back felt as if it were on fire. There was no way of knowing if he was staring at her the way she imagined he was, but the uncertainty made it all the more unnerving. Why had she agreed to wear one of Sir Patrick's daughter's gowns instead of the one she was carrying in her saddlebags? The velvet dress was cut more daringly than the ones she was used to wearing and felt rather tight, hugging her in all the places men liked to caress with their gazes, making her body desperate to be touched in a way it would never have, had she been wearing her own, more serviceable gown.

Or perhaps she was just deluding herself. Perhaps her desire to be stroked had nothing to do with the deep blue dress, and all to do with the provocative Laird Campbell. The man was too distracting by half, and the moment they had spent alone in the darkness the other night had proved he posed a real danger to her resolve to be a good wife to Dougal.

Was he looking at her? Her nipples, at least, had already assumed he was. They had hardened, as if trying to pierce through the precious fabric. Without looking she felt sure the nubs would be visible under the velvet. Oh well, should anyone remark on it, she could always blame the chilly atmosphere of the church. She shook her head. What was she thinking? Of course no one would say a word about the state of her nipples! The only person she knew who would dare to comment on such a scandalous thing was Cameron and there would be no hiding the truth from him. Even if she lied, she had a suspicion that he would know the truth, namely that *he*, and not the cold, was responsible for the way her body was responding. Because it wasn't just her nipples and her breasts that were taut with need. The place between her legs had grown hot and slick.

Bethan shifted on the pew slightly, trying to ease the burning. Damn and blast, how long would the mass last? She couldn't remember a christening ever being that long. In the state she was in, this was akin to torture.

"Are you all right?" Janet, Sir Patrick's daughter murmured in her ear as the congregation was preparing to sing yet another hymn. "You seem agitated."

Agitated. Yes. That was one word for it.

"Forgive me. I have a slight headache, that's all."

That was a lie, but what else could she say?

I'm getting in a state imagining my betrothed's uncle's heated gaze on me and wishing it was his hands. Can't you see the way my nipples have peaked? And it is nothing compared to the need burning between my legs.

"I'm sorry to hear it," Janet said, sitting back down once the song had ended. "When this is over, I will ask my aunt Beatrice to give you one of her potions. They work wonders on me."

"Thank you, I'm sure that will help."

Bethan already knew the potion would be of no use. The throbbing was not situated in her temples but much lower, and only one thing would make it better. As, unfortunately, pushing Cameron to the floor and impaling herself on his hardness was out of the question, she had no other choice but to wait. Eventually, her body would heed what reality was telling it, and the need for him would go away.

Yes... It had to go away eventually. There was no other choice.

Cameron congratulated himself on his choice of seat. From where he was, he had a clear view of Bethan, and he could not take his eyes from the beguiling sight. His superior height allowed him to see most of her, even though she was surrounded by a sea of women. The velvet dress she was wearing exposed more of her shoulders than the gown she'd been wearing for riding, revealing skin that was just as flawless as the silk of her cheeks. A beauty spot placed in the crook of her neck as if to lure men in, dared him to put his lips over it and bite. A long, glossy chestnut lock had escaped from her complicated coiffure and brushed her skin every time she turned her head. It was maddening.

In fact, everything about her that day was maddening.

The cut of the dress Sir Patrick's daughter had lent her emphasized the sensual swell of her hips and he gave a grunt when his lower body manifested its unequivocal approval. He was in a church, damn it, he could not get hard now! But how could he stop himself when she looked like the most mouthwatering offering? The blue of the velvet was exactly the shade he would have chosen to make her skin appear the color of cream. He scowled. Thinking about food now wouldn't help.

It would only tempt him to devour something that he had no right to.

Instead, he allowed his gaze to wander up and down her spine. She was standing very erect, as if she thought she might be under scrutiny. Well, she certainly was. He suspected that he wouldn't be the only man watching her and he wasn't best pleased with the idea. Sir Patrick had said that the women outnumbered the men, and it was certainly true, but there were still more than enough men around, men who no doubt delighted in admiring her.

"Lady Bethan has never looked better, don't you think?" Angus murmured, leaning toward him when they sat back down again.

"She's not a lady," was all Cameron could answer. The other option was to agree, and he feared that if he did, he would reveal just how alluring he found her in the blue dress.

"Aye, well, she should be. Pity Dougal could not rally men to his cause, and thus did not succeed the old laird. Then, as his wife, she would have been Lady Campbell."

Was the man determined to have his nose broken? Cameron bunched his fists. He cared not to be reminded that Bethan was set to marry his nephew; he was having a hard enough time trying to forget it. Only the fact that they were currently attending mass prevented him from grabbing Angus by the collar and hoisting him up in the air to relieve his frustration.

"Do you think you could stop bothering me with your

unhelpful comments?" he growled, keeping his gaze on the priest in front of him.

Angus inhaled sharply, as if suddenly realizing how his words could be interpreted. He had inadvertently hinted that he thought it wrong for Cameron to have been chosen in his nephew's stead. "Of course, I-I didn't mean anything by it," he stammered, worried his laird would think him disloyal, "only that the lady deserved to be married to a man who allows her to become—"

"I know what you meant, and I'm telling you again, cease your useless blabbering or you will find yourself tasting my knuckles as soon as the ceremony is over. My hand is itching something fierce."

As was his groin. But that was another matter, and not something Angus could do anything about.

"Aye, my laird."

When everyone started to make their way to the doors, Cameron realized he had barely heard a word the priest had said. Never had a christening seemed so short.

Chapter Six

Who on earth had thought it a good idea to place her so far away from Cameron? Bethan stared at her empty cup of ale, feeling dejected. She had been with him almost constantly in the last week and it felt odd to not even be able to see him.

The meal was nearly over, thankfully. Next to her a tall, blond man who'd introduced himself as one of Sir Patrick's numerous cousins, was describing the merits of flailed maces over regular flanged ones in combat. Under normal circumstances such a discussion would not have stirred the least spark of interest within her but, with her mind full of thoughts of Cameron, she was one anecdote away from breaking the habit of a lifetime and escaping mid-conversation. Only her unshakable politeness made it impossible for her to simply stand up and leave.

In her place, of course, Cameron wouldn't have hesitated to tell the man he was boring him. She found herself jealous of his ability to be blunt and to the point. How much time and energy she would save if she could just follow his example. Maybe it was only self-preservation that made him send annoying people to hell. He was only trying to preserve his sanity. It seemed a very wise choice right now.

When the music started Sir Alan was still doing his best to engage her attention. Mercifully, he had stopped describing the damage that could be inflicted on a human body with lethal weapons. Instead, he started to whisper compliments into her ear. Bethan cringed. This was way, way worse than descriptions of smashed human skulls. Evidently, he had mistaken her compliance during the banquet for interest on her part and the gleam in his eyes made it clear he thought her already won over.

"I will say that poor Janet never wore that velvet dress the way you do," he purred, his gaze fastening on the bodice edge framing her breasts. It was admittedly quite low, but did he really have to eye her up so shamelessly? "She doesn't have such sweet fruits to offer so perhaps it is no surprise."

Go drapia. In a moment he would tell her he wanted to peel the dress off her and taste those "sweet fruits." The thought of his lips sliding over her skin gave her the courage she needed.

"I'm sorry, my lord, but being betrothed, I'm sure I should not consent to have men whispering tender words into my ears."

"Betrothed?" He sounded as if he was choking on the nut he'd just popped into his mouth.

"Yes. I am even now on my way to Scotland, where I will be married to a man from a powerful clan, Dougal Campbell." This blasted betrothal was at last proving to offer some advantage. "Didn't Sir Patrick tell you?"

"No, he didn't," Sir Alan said slowly. And, to her relief, he straightened back up, his eyes on her face once more.

The satisfaction of having put a stop to his unwelcome advances was quickly replaced by annoyance, however. From prospective seducer, he appointed himself as protector of her virtue, scowling at every man bold enough to even look her way. She clenched her teeth and waited for the musicians to start playing. Surely it could not be too long before she was finally free of him.

At long last, the servants began to clear the table, leaving only the plates of sweetmeats and jugs of spiced wine in front of the guests. Sir Alan glanced at the musicians who were tuning their instruments and tilted his head in consideration. Bethan tensed up. As soon as they struck the first chord, he would ask her to dance, she could just feel it. She had to get out of there before it was too late.

Luckily, Cameron had left his seat and was now standing on the other side of the hall, talking to a man who was sporting an impressive beard. Straightening her shoulders, she improvised.

"I'm sorry, I will have to leave you now that the meal is over. I see Laird Campbell, my betrothed's uncle, by the door and I have a message from one his men to deliver to him."

"Surely it can wait a moment? The music is about to start."

"I'm afraid not. As he was talking to the priest earlier, I didn't dare disturb him, but he's been anxious to get that message. He is quite an overbearing man and will only come and get me if I don't go to him now that he is free. Surely you understand that I don't want to give him or my betrothed cause to reproach me?"

Bethan repressed a smile, delighted with herself. The lie had passed her lips more easily than she would have suspected. This was easier than she had thought.

Or...perhaps it was not, if people were going to ignore what she said.

"Come," Sir Alan said, filling her cup with more wine. It was as if she had not spoken. "You don't need to be afraid of the man, demanding though he might be. He's hardly going to run you through with his sword for a small delay."

No, but I might crush your skull with a flailed mace in a

moment, Bethan thought savagely. *I hear they are superior to the flanged ones.*

"I'm sorry, but I really should go before he comes to get me. He can really turn quite nasty, as I've learned to my cost," she said, addressing her mental apologies to Cameron who, she suspected, did not have a cruel bone in his body. Being formidable was one thing, nasty quite another.

Deciding it was the only way to convince Sir Alan of her intentions, she stood up.

He rose in turn, and she quickly understood he was not merely being gallant. He meant to follow her.

"That's it. I've heard enough of this Lord Campbell. Worry not, if he wants to take issue with you, this time he will have to contend with me first."

Without further ado, he started to lead her in the direction of the door. Dismay washed through Bethan. This was why she never lied, because it only created problems! Why had she painted Cameron in such a bad light? Why had she pretended she needed to see him at all? Couldn't she have done what a normal person would do, and said she needed to see to her personal needs? Or even better, tell Sir Alan the truth, namely that she was bored out of her mind in his presence? Everyone else she knew would not have given it another thought. Instead, she had dug herself and possibly Cameron, too, into a hole, and she had no idea how to get out of it.

"Please, this isn't necessary," she whispered, panicked at the idea of the scene to come. The man was taking his role as protector ridiculously seriously and it could only end badly, in humiliation or anger.

"I beg to differ. I will not have you face the monster on your own. Where is he?"

"Over there, talking to the man in the green t-tunic," Bethan stammered. After the disaster created by her first lie, she could not think of another.

"Oh." Sir Alan slowed down, obviously daunted by Cameron's commanding presence. It was hard to blame him. The Scot had never looked more intimidating than he did tonight, dressed in black from his fiery-crowned head to his boot-clad toes. She had the impression that if she'd made it clearer who her betrothed's uncle was before, her self-appointed defender would have passed on the chance to accompany her to face the "monster." Which would have suited just fine.

But unfortunately, with his credibility as a heroic man at stake, he couldn't back down. He walked bravely on and stopped behind Cameron, ready to stand his ground.

There was no time to lose. Bethan spoke quickly, before he could tell them he was not expecting any messages and ruin everything.

"My laird, Murdo bade me to speak to you without delay." When he turned around, she did her best to convey with her eyes that he was expected to go along with the pretense. Would he understand? "Do you have a moment?"

Cameron raised an eyebrow in surprise and no wonder. They both knew Murdo was unlikely to use her to deliver his messages. She was no menial. Before he could answer, however, Sir Alan spoke.

"My lord, this young lady here tells me that you have something important to discuss with her but surely it can wait. The music has just started, and I was about to ask her to join the dance."

He managed to sound both patronizing and pompous, a disastrous combination. Bethan knew that even if Cameron hadn't wanted to help her before, he would now, just to put the man back into his place. She breathed a discreet sigh of relief and braced herself for the onslaught.

"Being Scottish, and not English, I prefer to be addressed as 'my laird,' as you just heard." He paused and seemed to grow even taller. "And how should I address you, pray tell? I'm afraid I have no idea who you might be."

"I'm Sir Alan," the man supplied in a much less confident manner.

"Well, Sir Alan, unfortunately no, my discussion with Bethan can't wait. I would have thought that she, or I, would be in a better position to appreciate this than you, but you evidently thought differently."

"I only meant—"

"I know what you meant, thank you. My grasp of your language is more than sufficient." Eyes glittering like crystals, he offered his arm to Bethan. Utterly under his spell, she took it. "Don't worry, though," he carried on, his gaze once again on Sir Alan, "I promise to release the lady the moment she expresses the wish to return to you. In the meantime, I suggest you find yourself another dancing partner. It should not be too difficult. As you can see, women abound tonight."

Throwing an apologetic glance at a bemused Sir Alan, Bethan followed him.

To her surprise, however, instead of turning to the door, he led her straight to the middle of the hall, where people were twirling in time to the music. She had expected him to take her outside in the lists and in all honesty, a breath of fresh air would have been welcome. The atmosphere in the hall was heavy with spices, sweat and smoke, and after having endured Sir Alan's blabbering for what felt like an eternity, she was suddenly seized by the desire to be alone with Cameron in the cool darkness, like the other night.

"I have no wish to dance," she whispered, both relieved he had played along with her scheme and confused at the vehemence he'd displayed. He had been twice as intimidating as usual, and made sure to speak in a near unintelligible accent, a far cry from the burr that usually charmed her ear. If she didn't know better, she would have thought Sir Alan was one of his enemies. But surely the two men had not met before?

"Too bad you don't want to dance, as that is precisely what we'll be doing," Cameron answered, joining the circle of dancers who were getting ready for another carole.

The moment his fingers closed on her right hand she averted her gaze. Though they were dancing in a round at least twenty people strong, the contact felt impossibly intimate. When she froze, the man to her left took her other hand and smiled at her encouragingly. He evidently thought she was nervous at the idea of following steps she didn't know. She wasn't, even if admittedly, she had never been the best dancer. Instead, she was panicked everyone, including Cameron himself, would see how disturbing she found it to be held by the brooding Scot.

The music started. For a moment, Bethan focused on mimicking the movements of the people opposite her, then once she felt comfortable, she turned to face Cameron. It had just occurred to her that if she appeared flushed, she could blame it on the dancing.

"You enjoyed humiliating the man, didn't you?" she chided in a low voice.

Cameron let out a grunt that could equally have been a laugh or a scoff. "And here I was thinking that you would thank me for going along with your scheme when I could easily have exposed your shameful lie. Deliver a message from Murdo, indeed! What did he ask you to tell me that he could not tell me himself, I wonder?"

The urge to tease him was so overwhelming she didn't even

try to resist it. "He asked me to inform you he had gone to the nearest tavern, in search of a willing woman, as he's tired of using his callused hands to see to his needs."

This time she recognized the grunt for what it was. Amusement. Or possibly shock. And no wonder. What had possessed her to jest about what she had seen that night at the tavern? They had agreed not to talk about it, had they not? And yet here she was, being unforgivably brazen.

Cameron leaned in toward her, his heat warming her cheek. "Well, be sure to tell Murdo next time you see him that I need not know how and where he gets his relief. The less I think about it, the better."

Bethan's heart leaped at his answer. How she loved it when they jested together! "I will."

Just then the music picked up pace, and for a moment they were prevented from talking.

"Why did you tell Sir Alan you would let me go back to him when I wanted to?" Bethan asked once the rhythm had slowed down once more. She'd had time to come back to her senses and realized she should steer the conversation away from men seeking relief. "You know full well I have no intention of doing so."

"Do I?" Cameron's lips quivered.

"Yes, you do," she scolded. "And so, when I don't, he will understand that I found him dull."

He frowned. "What of it? If you did find him dull, why shouldn't you let him know it? But, of course, if you wish to go back to him after this dance you are free to do so, as I said." The clasp around her fingers tightened, contradicting the words. Bethan swallowed. Dare she hope he wanted her to stay with him?

"No, I—I mean, yes, I did find him dull. How could I not? All he kept talking about was maces, how flailed ones were better than flanged ones, or the other way around, and how they could reduce a man's skull to a pulp. It was horrid, really, but I... I could not make him understand..."

Too confused, she stopped talking. Cameron's body was so hard and hot next to hers, he smelled so good, a smell evocative of something like cut grass and fresh air, he sounded so masculine, and he looked so intense that it was all too much. Everything started to go awry. Her mind was spinning out of control, her senses were overwhelmed, her mouth had gone dry, her chest had tightened.

"What are you trying to say, Bethan?"

It was the first time he had called her Bethan, and she had no idea how he managed to make the name she had heard so many times before sound so seductive.

"I meant that yes, of course, the man was dull. That is precisely why I wanted to escape. I just hadn't dreamed he would want to save me from my betrothed's demanding, insufferably high-handed uncle."

"Ah. So that is the role I was supposed to play. Thanks. I was wondering." He smiled and arched a brow at the same time, a lethal look. "Demanding and insufferably high-handed. Mm. I can make my peace with it. I have been called worse things."

Her heart fluttered again, because she enjoyed it when he teased her almost as much as she liked it when they jested together. "I thought that if I made you sound like an overbearing monster, he would not follow me," she explained.

"Then you have a lot to learn about men. Once they have set their eyes on a woman, they don't take it too well to have her snatched away from them."

He growled, and the sound reverberated to the bottom of Bethan's soul. His fingers tightened further, making her wonder if he was subconsciously making sure no one would snatch her away from him either.

"I told Sir Alan I was betrothed precisely because I did not want him to entertain any ideas about me," she defended. "How was I to know he would start acting all proprietary instead?"

"As I said, you have a lot to learn about men."

The irony of the comment was not lost on her. Up until that moment Bethan would have sworn she was more knowledgeable on the subject than the average unmarried woman. But Cameron made her feel like a novice indeed. His transparent eyes bore into her, the expression in them impossibly intense. She shivered. What could she say? Nothing. Her tongue was glued to the roof of her mouth.

She carried on dancing.

"Listen," Cameron said after a while, his tone serious once more. "The music is about to stop. We had better make it look as if we were deep in conversation when it does, otherwise I fear the esteemed Sir Alan will try his hand at rescuing you from the overbearing Scot."

Indeed, the man was eyeing her up in concern from the corner of the room, as if worried she was being mistreated. The idea of leaving Cameron to go back to him was simply too dire to contemplate. She wouldn't put it past him to resume his bloodcurdling description of weapons of war, or talk about the "sweet fruits" she was hiding under her gown. She had no idea which would be worse.

"Please," she said in a breath. "Do whatever you have to do to make him understand that you will not hand me over to anyone."

Hand her over to anyone.

Cameron barely repressed a growl. Indeed, he would not. The interminable banquet without Bethan had been torture, and now that they had finally been reunited, he would keep her by his side for the rest of the evening. His fingers tightened their grip around hers of their own accord, the connection between them searing. Damn and blast, he had to stop doing this, or her hand would end up being reduced to a pulp. Every time he'd mentioned her leaving him during the carole, he'd involuntarily squeezed her fingers, as if to stop her from going anywhere.

"On what grounds could I possibly want to keep you for myself, Bethan?" he purred in her ear, unable to resist the temptation of leaning closer. Perhaps she wouldn't see anything amiss in the gesture. Hadn't he just said they were supposed to appear deep in conversation? That's all they were doing.

"Why are you suddenly calling me Bethan?" she asked instead of answering.

"Because it's your name."

It was beautiful, like her—and he liked using it. It was intimate, the only intimacy they were allowed to share. He wished she would start calling him Cameron, instead of "my laird." That was his title, not who he was. With her, he wanted to be himself. He wanted to hear her say his name in her delicious Welsh accent. He wanted to hear her whisper it in his ear when she begged him to fuck her, moan it when he pleasured her with his mouth first, scream it at the top of her lungs when he finally gave her what she wanted and hammered into her.

Damn, damn, *damn!* Why was he doing this to himself? Not only was she not for him but they were in the middle of a crowded room, and he was wearing a very short tunic. If he didn't put a stop to his musings in the instant, everyone would see more of him than they wanted.

"Yes, Bethan is m-my name," she stammered, as if she had not realized it before. Or perhaps she had seen something flash in his eyes and guessed that a shard of desire had just split his groin.

Without warning, and before he could say anything, the music stopped. The onlookers burst into applause, the dancer to Bethan's left released her with a bow. When she faced him square on, she appeared slightly dazed. Automatically, his right hand encircled her left wrist. *Mo chreach!* It was so small, so delicate. It made something inside of him melt, a completely new sensation. Usually she stirred his anger, his protective instinct, or his lust. But never this...tenderness, for want of a better word.

Oh, and the way she was looking at him! Her eyes were wide, her lips were parted, her cheeks were flushed, and she seemed incapable of coherent thought. He dared not think how *he* would look right now. If how he felt was any indication, she would certainly take fright.

"You haven't answered my question," he said at long last. "Why should I want to keep you with me?"

Who was he asking the question to, her or himself? He had no idea, but he dearly wanted to hear what she had to say, as they both knew she did not belong to him, she was not his to guard, and he should not want to keep her with him at all times. Heart hammering hard in his chest, Cameron waited, hoping Bethan would come up with an answer that would help him see how ludicrous he was being for wanting to spend his time with her.

She took in a deep breath, as if steeling herself for something she found unpleasant. "I-I don't know why. I'd understand if you preferred to go speak to someone else now that the carole is over. But please, will you first—"

"No." He would prefer nothing other than being with her. And he would not let that wretched Sir Alan get her back in his clutches. "Don't worry. I won't let you die of boredom with Sir Alan."

Let the man try to take her away from him if he dared. He would soon discover that when applied properly, a punch from a determined man could match the best of maces for effect.

Wrapping her hand on the crook of his elbow, he led her toward the door.

"Come. Methinks it's time for me to act like the insufferably high-handed monster I'm supposed to be and take you out of here."

~

"Now what do we do?"

From her vantage point on the battlements, Bethan looked into the distance, to the line of dark trees piercing the sky, making the usually flat horizon appear jagged. Had everything been torn part today? She certainly felt nothing like her usual self, had not for a week. Since she had set eyes on Cameron Campbell that night by the gate, her life had been ripped into shreds. She did not see how it would ever go back to normal now.

Was it even possible, considering that in less than two weeks she would be married to a stranger? Her life had been irremediably altered, whether she liked it or not.

Well, for now she was here, so she had better make the most of the reprieve.

True to his word, Cameron had dragged her all the way across the bailey to the west battlements with the air of someone who would not be denied, adding credence to the tale that he was the demanding, unreasonable man she had claimed him to be. They were now well away from all the activity—and Sir Alan and his blasted maces. She could breathe at last. Though to passersby she would appear to be taking the air in the company of her betrothed's uncle, the furious beatings of her heart made it clear that things were not as innocent as they appeared. She was alone in the dark with a man she desired like she had not desired anyone else, and she wasn't sure she would stop him if by some miracle he decided to draw her into his arms and kiss her into surrender.

For she couldn't be the only one feeling the tension between them, could she?

"We'll wait here a while, and if anyone comes too close, we will pretend to be arguing," Cameron answered her question calmly. "If we play our part well, no one will want to interfere, believe me, least of all your Sir Alan. You're safe as long as you're with me."

Mm. Safe from what, Bethan wondered? She looked at the torch burning bright by the gate some distance away. The flickering flames seemed to mirror the fluttering sensations dancing in her chest. Though in the darkness she could barely see Cameron, she could feel him, smell him, sense him.

"So. It seems you were telling the truth after all," he said, fingering the hilt of his sword as if he'd seen an invisible enemy.

"The truth? What do you mean?"

"You do spend your time being harassed by men. Was Sir Alan the only one after you tonight, I might ask?"

"I'm afraid I do not know. While he was detailing the most gruesome ways of smashing a man's skull to pieces, he didn't leave any opportunity for anyone else to get a word in edgeways, myself included," she answered with spirit. The notion that she could have spent the evening with Cameron instead, and gotten to know him better, made her angry. What a waste of time this banquet had been. "Once I informed him of my pending wedding, it was even worse. Having appointed himself as protector of my virtue, he did not allow anyone to get within twenty feet of me."

"A wonderful evening, then."

She snorted. "Wonderful, indeed. It made me wish I had a mace with which to try out all the things I've learned tonight."

Cameron gave a throaty laugh, and she realized that she had

only seen him laugh like this with her. During his dealings with Lord Sheridan, he'd been efficient and to the point. At Castell y Ddraig, with her brother, he'd done his best to appear reassuring. With his men he was focused and commanding, and he'd been affable but somewhat distant with Sir Patrick. Only with her did he allow himself to relax.

She loved it, because it allowed her to do the same, and be herself.

"What about you?" she asked. "I imagine that you had to fend off women's advances all evening? With men in such short supply, you must have been besieged."

Although... Had there been ten times as many men present tonight, a man like him would still have stood out and been a target of choice for the ladies.

Cameron gave an exaggerated sigh. "As a matter of fact, I was besieged, as you say. Fortunately, my extensive experience in the art of rebuking women made the task of keeping them at bay easy. Lady Cecily was very persistent, though."

Sir Patrick's wife's younger sister, he meant, next to whom he'd been sitting. A woman a few years his senior, widowed but still a beauty, she would have begged her sister to place their handsome guest next to her during the banquet. What had the two of them talked about? Not flanged maces, that much was certain. Had Cameron surrendered to her wiles and agreed to go find her in bed later tonight? Jealousy pierced Bethan's gut at the thought. But why would he refuse her invitation? They were both free to act on the desire they felt, unlike her.

"Her name is Lady Cecilia I think," she murmured, looking straight at him. The moon crescent had come out from behind the clouds, and she could now see his face better.

"Is it? It's possible. I'll admit that I wasn't paying too much attention to what she was saying," Cameron confided, leaning in toward her.

"How rude of you!" She made a point of chiding him but secretly, she was pleased the woman interested him so little that he didn't even remember her name.

"Aye. Positively scandalous." He straightened back up and crossed his arms over his chest—his very broad, perfect chest. "But tell me, apart from maces, what did our friend Sir Alan talk to you about?"

She reddened, understanding what he was trying to do. "Very well. You've made your point. I did not attend to what he was saying either." She guessed, rather than saw, Cameron's smirk. "You know, you should give me some advice about how to get rid of undesirable suitors, seeing as you are quite the expert at it. What *do* you do to repel them?"

Instead of answering he eyed her up a long moment. "Whatever I do would be of no use to you I'm afraid, Bethan."

Again, the use of her name, like a warm caress on her senses. She could not find it in herself to protest, even if she perhaps should. It felt right to hear him use it.

"Why is that?"

"Because for a set down to work, you have to mean it and I'm afraid that you do not have a ruthless bone in your delectable little body." Delectable? She barely had time to absorb the impact of the word before he carried on. "You are also far too concerned by what people might think and what is proper to be honest. Fortunately, I don't suffer from the same problem." His mouth twitched, an obvious attempt at hiding a smile.

"You're right," she mumbled, feeling dejected. She did not have what it took. "I'm too weak to make it work."

"That's not quite what I said. And I do not think you weak, not in the least."

She was taken aback by the comment. He seemed to say that she shouldn't change the way she was, even if it meant that she could not get rid of undesirable people when she needed it. This, right after he had called her body delectable, was enough to transform her insides into gruel.

"I'm easily embarrassed," she clarified, "something I know couldn't happen to you."

"Why is that?"

Cameron was curious. Bethan had given his character a lot of thought, if she thought she knew what could or not could happen to him. The notion pleased him, because he, too, had spent a lot of time thinking about her in the last week. It was the first time they were talking so openly. He had explained to her why he hadn't wanted to become laird the other night, but this felt a lot more personal. They were discussing their characters, not their role in life. The distinction seemed important.

"I don't think you have much time for fools. If someone annoys you, like McBain, you turn them away in no uncertain terms." Was it a note of envy he detected in her voice? Perhaps. "Although, come to think of it, I suspect it would take a lot to upset you."

"Mm," he groaned. "You might be right there."

He wasn't particularly pleased by her observation, even if it was fair. Somehow it made him appear cold-hearted, which he hoped he was not. Her thinking of him as a remote, unfeeling individual was the last thing he wanted, because with her— toward her—he felt plenty.

But he realized she had meant the comment as a compliment, when she hastened to add, "You're lucky to be able to ignore what people think of you, is what I mean, and be honest. I wish I could do that."

"Maybe you overestimate my ability. I have been known to care about what people think on occasion."

He certainly cared about she thought of him.

"Oh. So, you are not as immune to criticism and self-doubt as we might think?" The idea seemed to please her.

"Of course not."

"And what sort of a man is my...Dougal?" she asked suddenly.

My Dougal. Though she hadn't meant it like that, Cameron's stiffened. The idea of Bethan leaving him to be married sent the now familiar shards of ice through his gut. The closer they came to Crois Dhubh the more unsettled he got.

"What are you asking? Are you afraid of meeting him?" It would make sense. His nephew was a stranger to her.

"Not precisely, but..." But she was. Her eyes were gleaming in the moonlight when she finally dared look at him. Say what she might, she *was* wary of what she would find in Scotland, understandably. "You know him. So, tell me. Should I be afraid of him?"

Dear God, he had to reassure her immediately. He could not imagine how he would feel in her place. She was about to meet a man who would effectively own her in the eyes of the law, and there was nothing she could do about it. Dougal could be a vicious tyrant and still there would be no escaping him. He could want to make her pay for not being the bride of his choice, he could slake his lust with her body night after night regardless of her wishes, he could hit her if she displeased him, and no one would be able to say anything. Well, he was laird, damn it, *he* would make sure he did say something if he ever saw her husband mistreating her. It was not just a question of honor, it was not just that he had promised her brother to look after her, it was...personal.

But he hoped it wouldn't come to that. As much as he disliked the idea of Bethan being married to his nephew, he knew he was not a bad man. It was only that he was not the man for her.

"You have nothing to be afraid of. Dougal is not a dangerous man. But I'm afraid he is not..." His voice trailed. What could he tell her? His nephew would never hurt her, granted, but he would never make her happy either. She needed a man, and Dougal was just a boy, full of dreams of grandeur and lacking the capacity to make them come true, unable to take care of a wife. "He's only twenty, so he can be forgiven for being a bit naïve sometimes," he finally said, deciding there was no point in being too honest. She would see the reality soon enough.

"I'm one and twenty, only a year older," she pointed out.

"Yes, you are."

But you are far wiser than your betrothed.

Cameron did not say the words. There was no need, she would have understood from his tone that was what he thought. Which was enough. There was a silence, then she spoke, her voice tentative.

"Is he experienced with women?"

The question surprised a cough out of him. Was she really trying to ascertain what kind of lover her future husband was? Though he'd guessed by now that she was not exactly like other women, more brazen and probably more knowledgeable about what happened in marital beds, her boldness was still unexpected. To think she'd just claimed to be too shy to be honest... With him, at least, she was not afraid to speak her mind. She had proved it on countless occasions.

"I think not," he said, doing his best not to dwell on the thought of her and Dougal in bed together. "As I said, he's still young, and untried in many respects. If you fear he will be a forceful, insatiable lover, then you need not—"

"I'm not afraid of that. But you see I...I'm not a virgin," she said in a breath.

The shocking, deeply personal admission tore through the air. Every muscle in Cameron's body stilled. Bethan was not a virgin? Now he understood why she had suddenly started asking about Dougal and his love life. She wanted to know whether she should fear his reaction when he found out his bride was not the innocent maiden he assumed her to be.

"Is this why you are nervous about your wedding night?" he asked in a growl. Imagining her in another man's arms was torture, especially because he had no idea what dark secret lurked in her past. It was not common for a woman who'd been betrothed before she was old enough to take interest in men to be experienced. So what had happened? Had she been forced or had she gone to a lover willingly? The first possibility sent his blood boiling with rage, and the second racing with lust.

"I never said that I was nervous about my wedding night," Bethan answered, raising her chin.

"You must be, why else would you confide to me that you are afraid of what your groom will say when he sees that you are not untouched?"

"Once again you are mistaking my intent. I'm not afraid of that."

He arched an eyebrow. Really the woman was, as he'd just thought, bold and unpredictable—and, apparently, even more knowledgeable than he had suspected. "What are you telling me then?"

Bethan bit her lip. What *was* she telling Cameron? Why was she discussing such private matters with him, even? It was not only awkward, but it could be dangerous, if he decided to use this information against her.

But she could not hold her tongue any longer. The closer they got to Scotland and finally meeting the man she would spend the rest of her life married to, the more nervous she became. And nothing Cameron had said about his nephew over the last few days had reassured her, least of all that he was as good as a virgin. She did not want to be married to someone who was even less mature than she was. She wanted a man who would treat her like his wife, not his sister, a lover who knew how to give her pleasure, not a boy looking at a mother-figure with puppyish adoration.

She stared into the horizon, wondering whether to be honest or not. In the end she decided to be. They had shared an unexpected moment of intimacy tonight, and she trusted that Cameron would understand.

"I am one and twenty. I have been betrothed for seven long years to a man I didn't choose and fear I might not like. From a young age I have been courted by men and last year I decided to take some to my bed," she said hurriedly. There. Let him know the full truth. It couldn't be worse from what he was imagining already. "I do not regret it, as I thought there was a distinct possibility my betrothed would find excuses to delay our wedding for another ten years or even cancel it altogether. After all, his father is not here to force him to honor a promise made when he was little more than a child and his life seems wholly devoted to Robert the Bruce. But apparently I was wrong, and he does want a wife. I don't blame him for it but now my marriage is fast approaching, and I am scared that my husband will not appeal to me, or..."

"Or satisfy you in bed as well as your lovers did," Cameron supplied with a taut smile. He didn't sound disapproving exactly, rather as if he shared her concerns. Her stomach sank another notch. Dear, oh, dear, that was not promising. He seemed to think Dougal would never give her what needed.

"Yes. The prospect is not an appealing one, because of course once I'm married, I intend to be faithful. I will not have any more lovers."

He nodded, then asked, his voice reduced to a growl. "How many have you had?"

Her heart skipped a beat. It sounded as if the idea

displeased him in the extreme. "That is none of your concern and hardly relevant. Or will you share with me the number of your conquests?"

"No, I won't, and you're right, it is none of my concern."

To Bethan's surprise, he did not point out that he, unlike her, was a man and as such not subjected to the restrictions that applied to her. As Dougal's uncle, and the man charged to deliver her safely to her betrothed, he would have been well within his rights to be outraged when she had announced that she was no virgin, but he had not so much as flinched. Even more surprisingly, he had understood her concerns about the satisfaction she was hoping to find in her husband's bed.

She waited, not knowing how to carry on this most unusual conversation. It was not every day that an unmarried woman discussed her past lovers with a member of her future husband's family. To add to her confusion, she was battling the urge to nestle herself into his arms, not in lust for once, but in gratitude. He had heard her shocking confession, and he had not judged, he had not roared in outrage, he had not made her feel dirty. Would Dougal be so understanding? Somehow, she doubted it.

Cameron was still reeling from Bethan's revelation. At least he had established that she had not been the victim of an assault. His mind had been put at rest, but his body was more inflamed than ever. Because, if she was not untouched and had already welcomed lovers to her bed then there would be no harm in the two of them—

He clenched his jaw so hard he heard a bone crack.

What was he thinking? No harm? Who was he fooling? The scope for disaster was endless. What if she fell with child? What if Dougal found out the uncle he'd entrusted with his wife's safety had seduced her? What if...

What if after having fallen in lust with her, he fell in love? At the moment it seemed too real a real risk, a risk he couldn't take because despite her revelation, nothing had changed. She was still going to marry his nephew.

"Are you going to tell Dougal?" Bethan asked in a low voice. Understandably, she was worried he would expose her. But it had not even crossed his mind to do so.

"No. This is between you and him, it has nothing to do with me," he said, fists bunched by his side. Would the boy even notice something was amiss? Not all virgins bled. If Bethan made sure to behave as she should and Dougal was a virgin himself, as Cameron suspected, and then he might not notice anything.

In any case, Cameron would not betray her. What purpose would it serve? She had said she intended to be faithful once she was married, and he believed her. If she was worried about having an unsatisfactory love life, it proved that she intended to welcome no other man than her husband in her bed. It was all that mattered.

"Wait, what were you doing that night at the tavern?" he asked suddenly. Had she gone in search of a man? His blood surged anew. "Tell me you did not seek your lovers amidst the customers—"

"No! I never sold my body, neither was I ever bedded by a man I did not choose!" Bethan sounded too horrified at the notion for him to doubt her words. "That night I had gone to... to..."

"You do not wish to tell me," he cut in when she faltered. "Don't."

He had learned far more than he could handle already. For days he had been fighting his desire for Bethan and now he was being told that he could have her without damaging her, that she had already taken lovers and wanted to be satisfied in bed... A woman like this was his every dream come true.

How on earth was he supposed to resist her now? Well, he

would just have to find a way, because he could *not* seduce his future niece by marriage, no matter what her past was.

"We will reach Crois Dhubh in less than two weeks," he said decisively. "You will soon meet your groom. All your questions will be answered."

And then they would part ways.

Yes. It was for the best.

Chapter Seven

In the end it took the retinue just a little over a fortnight to reach Crois Dhubh.

It had been the best and the worst two weeks of Bethan's life. Being with Cameron day and night was both a blessing and a torment because with each passing day, her feelings for him grew stronger. What had been little more than lust at first was evolving into something far more worrying, something she had not felt for any of the men who had taken possession of her body.

She feared that this Scot who had never even kissed her might have taken possession of her heart.

He'd taken to riding by her side instead of behind her and entertaining her with stories of his youth and she, in turn, had shared memories of her time spent with the Hunter family. It had been surprisingly soothing to recall those happy times.

The day they had crossed the border Murdo had been so relieved to be back on Scottish soil he'd burst into song. Soon, all the men had joined in, even Cameron. His voice was rich and true, warming her to the soul. Entranced, she had listened to songs in ancient Gaelic, and sworn to herself she would start learning the beautiful language at the first opportunity. Which was, she realized, right now. As they rode through a landscape of rolling purple hills and sparkling blue lakes, she had asked the men to teach her a few essential words. They had been only too delighted to help.

But as pleasant as it had been to ride through magical land in the company of men who had only her well-being at heart, she could not forget where they were headed and by the time they passed through the gate of Crois Dhubh, Bethan's nerves had been frayed to an unprecedented point. Her first glimpse of the place that was to be her home only added to her trepidation. It looked to be in a bad state of neglect. Used to the comfort of Castell Esgyrn and having seen what her brother had done at Castell y Ddraig, she could only despair at the contrast.

Oh, well, at least putting everything to rights would give her something to do.

They found an old man in the bailey, looking somewhat lost. When he saw Cameron dismount, his face lit up. Then he looked at her inquiringly, as if he had no idea who she was supposed to be. Her stomach fell another notch. Admittedly they had never met, but it would not be hard to guess who an unknown woman in the company of the laird might be. Didn't the people here know she was coming? Hadn't Dougal warned them?

"*Fàilte gu Crois Dhubh.*"

"He's welcoming you to Crois Dhubh," Cameron whispered in her ear. Bethan smiled her thanks, but she had understood the greeting. Then the man started to talk, his words coming too fast for her to even try to follow.

Cameron cut him short and answered in her stead. "*Béarla*" was the only word she recognized, because she had made sure it was one she learned, so as to ask people whether they could speak English or not upon meeting them. The man shook his head. Evidently, though he had been instructed to address her in English, he could not.

Dear God. Once the retinue had left, she would be left alone with people who could not understand her. It would happen soon enough. Cameron had been away from Nead an Diabhail for weeks. Eager to resume his responsibilities as laird, he would not linger here, but instead rush home at the first opportunity. It was hard to fight the sense of panic at the idea that they were soon to be parted.

"Please, I would like a moment to freshen up before I... before..."

Before I meet the man who is to be my husband.

Where was Dougal? Was he hiding in one of the rooms overlooking the bailey? Why hadn't he come to greet her? Was he even here? Or had he been called by the Bruce yet again? She hadn't imagined she would have to endure another delay.

"Of course. I'll have someone escort you."

Cameron looked preoccupied. What had the old man told him to cause him alarm? Had they been attacked while he'd been away? She had no idea, and she had enough on her mind to worry about this as well.

At a nod from his laird, Angus led her to a surprisingly clean and well-furnished bedchamber. It was clear the room had been aired and recently made ready. Bethan's spirits lifted marginally. At least some effort had been made to welcome her.

"Here you are, my lady." He looked worried as well, nothing like the jovial man she had come to know. What *was* going on?

"Thank you."

Once alone, she took every care with her appearance, smoothing the folds of her gown, shaking off the dust the journey, making sure to erase all trace of anguish on her face. The pounding of her heart though, she couldn't do anything about.

After waiting for so long, she was finally about to meet the man who would marry her on the morrow.

A knock on the door a moment later startled her.

"*Dewch i mewn.*" She was so startled she only realized too late that she had given the instruction to come in in Welsh. Still, she wasn't sure English would have been much better, and the meaning would be obvious.

A petite woman entered with a ewer of warm water and a piece of cloth. There was an odd look in her eyes. Diffidence? Pity? After placing everything on the table, she curtsied and retreated. Evidently, she didn't speak English either. The knot in Bethan's throat tightened another notch. How much worse could this get?

"*Tapadh leat,*" she thanked the woman, who was already closing the door.

Well, no use in lingering unnecessarily. She had better get on with the task of making herself presentable. There was no doubt the water and cloth had been sent by Cameron, who always saw to her comfort.

Before leaving the room she took in a deep, fortifying breath. This was it. Feeling absurdly like the fourteen-year-old girl she had been when her wedding contract had been signed, she stepped out into the spiral staircase. She promised herself she would write to Gwenllian as soon as she could, and tell her all about her groom, in the hope that she would be able to reassure her friend.

In the courtyard she found a small group of men talking, predictably, in indecipherable, rapid Gaelic. Cameron was nowhere to be seen. Angus, Murdo and Hamish had also disappeared. Everything within her roiled. Surely they had not left already, without ensuring she was all right first, without saying goodbye?

She walked over to the men, making herself as tall as she

could. Soon to be mistress of the place, she had better start as she meant to go on. She could not be seen as hesitant or frightened.

"Does anyone here speak English?" she asked, bracing herself for their blank looks of incomprehension. "*Béarla?*"

All eyes turned to a tall man who, despite his tall stature, seemed to be no older than she was. Her heart skipped a beat. Could this be Dougal Campbell? If he was, then she was pleased to see that her first reaction to him was not one of revulsion. He seemed quite personable.

"I do," he said with obvious reluctance. It was not hard to guess he would have liked nothing better than to have someone else deal with her, but seeing as he was the only one capable of talking to her, he had no choice but to volunteer. "Rory McIntosh, at your service."

Ah. So not Dougal then. Her heart plummeted.

"Where is Laird Campbell?"

Let him be still here, please.

"He's...talking to the steward."

"Well, I'm ready. Please take me to his nephew, Dougal." Better to get this over with as soon as possible.

Silence met her request.

"I'm so sorry, my lady. The old laird's son..." The man floundered, looked helplessly around him. Unsurprisingly, no one offered any help. "I'm afraid Dougal Campbell is dead."

Chapter Eight

Dead.

Arms wrapped tight around her middle, Bethan stared at the altar in front of her without seeing anything, just like she had all those years ago at Sheridan Manor, when William had asked her what was wrong. She felt just as at a loss now than she had felt then.

Her husband was dead. Or rather, the boy she had been betrothed to for so long would never marry her. Her father's machinations had all been for naught. Her situation was unchanged. The twenty-one-year-old woman she'd become was in just as hopeless a situation as her fourteen-year-old self had been.

They had buried Dougal the day before, the morning after their arrival, in other words, on the day he should have married her. His death had preceded the retinue's arrival by less than half a day. Had they not stayed for Sir Patrick's niece's christening, Bethan would have made it in time to meet him, perhaps even marry him on his deathbed. She could not help but think it would have been better, if admittedly grim. As a widow, she would have been afforded considerably more leeway than as an undesirable, penniless virgin expected to be chaste. As Dougal Campbell's widow, her future would have been assured, perhaps even her happiness. No one would have minded if she went back home or even remarried. She would have been free.

If only it had not rained that day, if only they not taken refuge in Sir Patrick's castle, if only they had not accepted his invitation or had not—

No.

Bethan put an abrupt halt on her wayward thoughts. Dwelling on them could only cause her pain. What was done was done, and poor Dougal was dead, killed by a bloody flux contracted during the retreat from Dublin, where Robert the Bruce and his men had gone to reenforce his brother Edward's army.

She hadn't even known he'd gone there in the winter. No doubt this also accounted for his decision to send Cameron to get her. He'd thought to rest for a while after another hard campaign and finally set his affairs in order. Instead, he'd gotten eternal sleep.

Footsteps were heard behind her. Bethan stiffened and turned around. Master McDuff, the castle steward, was walking up the aisle, oblivious to her presence in the shadows. He came to a halt when he saw her. She had sat at the end of the pew, as close to the wall as she could.

"Forgive me for interrupting, I didn't know you had come here to engage in private prayer," he said, coming closer. "You must be devastated."

Bethan lowered her gaze to hide her reaction. She hadn't come here to pray, but to be alone, to hide and be with her thoughts. As to being devastated... Was that what she was feeling?

She pursed her lips when the answer hit her. No, she was not devastated. Rather, she felt oddly empty. All this time spent waiting for something that would never happen, all these pointless preparations, these crushed hopes, these never-ending questions, these sleepless nights now felt like a waste of time.

Be careful what you wish for.

After years spent wishing her betrothed would break the contract signed by their fathers, she had gotten what she wanted. Fate had ensured in the cruelest way that she would never be Dougal Campbell's wife. She could have laughed if her freedom had not cost the poor man his life.

"We had no idea where you had gone but the laird is looking for you," the steward told her quietly.

Bethan nodded. She had guessed he would be. They had not spoken since the moment she had retired to her bedchamber after having buried Dougal. Cameron would be wondering how she was.

"Ask him to join me here," she said, standing up. In the cold of the church, her limbs had started to stiffen.

"Of course."

It wasn't long before the door of the little chapel opened behind her. The sound of hard boots on stone, such a masculine sound, heralded Cameron's arrival. It suddenly occurred to her that for the first time she would face him as a free woman. How would they behave? Heart thudding hard in her chest, she bunched her fists and turned to look at him.

Jesus. Had he always been so manly? Yes. But this time there was a gleam in his eyes she had never seen before, one she could not make sense of.

"You wanted to see me?" she asked, deciding it would be better for her peace of mind if she didn't know why he was looking at her in that way.

"Yes."

He did not offer any explanation, didn't move a muscle. His face betrayed nothing. She waited.

"My condolences," she said eventually. "Dougal was your nephew. I imagine that you must feel his loss keenly." Perhaps that was the reason behind his unusual behavior. A member of Dougal's family, he would be more affected by his death than she was.

Cameron sighed, looking slightly caught out. "I didn't really know the boy."

"And I never even saw him!" she cried, unable to stop herself. At last, the emotions boiling under the surface erupted. "I don't even know what he looked like!" This was ludicrous. How could she mourn a stranger? The two of them had no memories together. She wasn't even sure she could pretend to feel grief. Fortunately, Cameron didn't seem to require it of her.

"I know. You do not have to pretend to be sad with me. I understand. Dougal was nothing to you, his death has left you cold."

The blunt statement did not shock her, for it was nothing but the truth. It felt good to have someone else acknowledge it without any judgment. And he was right. The boy lying in his grave was nothing to her.

Perhaps that was why she felt so out of sorts, because the situation was anything but normal.

"Yes. And I was nothing to him. His father shackled him to me when he was too young to even think about marriage. In all this time, he never made any effort to come and see me, he wrote to me only twice, years ago, two brief notes that revealed nothing of the man he'd been. I always came second, or even third in his mind, after his loyalty to the Bruce and his country!" she said fiercely, as resentment, bitterness, fear for the future poured out of her. "He never spared a thought about me, all these years. Why should I mourn him? Why should I care when he never showed me any mark of interest? He would not have recognized me had we found ourselves face to face with each other in the middle of a room, me, the woman he was supposed to spend his life with! I left my country for nothing, I worried for nothing, and now I have nothing."

All anger spent, Bethan fell on the nearest pew.

Slowly, tears started to flow down her cheeks. As dissatisfactory as the arrangement had been, she had imagined herself married to Dougal for what seemed like forever, and it was hard to imagine an alternative.

"What will happen to me?" she said, lowering her head in defeat.

Instead of answering, Cameron sat down next to her—and drew her into his arms. She tried to fight him off at first and then she allowed herself to relent, telling herself that he would not let her get away anyway. He was so warm, so strong, his embrace was so comforting, and she had wanted to feel his arms around her for so long that she could not resist.

For a long moment he just held her, allowing her to ease some of the weight crushing her chest by crying. She had desperately needed the release so she was grateful.

"I will tell you what will happen to you," he murmured in her ear when her tears finally abated. "You will marry a man of your choosing, instead of being shackled to a stranger who never showed any interest in you."

"How? No respectable man will want me. I have no fortune or land. I am no longer a virgin. I am old."

Against her cheek she felt Cameron's chest vibrate and it took her a moment to understand that he was laughing. How could he laugh at a time like this? "Old? You cannot be a day over fifty! You still have all your teeth, and from I can see when you scowl at me, they are reasonably straight."

Fifty! Bethan would have drawn back in outrage had it not been obvious that he was mocking her to make her feel better. To her surprise, it did. Being mocked by Cameron was oddly soothing. There was a tenderness in his voice when he spoke, and his arms had tightened around her as if in protection.

"Teeth, be they reasonably straight, is not what men are looking for in a bride," she said weakly, her face still buried in his chest.

Her beauty meant that men would not stop looking at her, but with only one purpose in mind—to take her to bed, not to the altar. They would only ever want her as a leman, not a wife.

"There is only one thing men will ever want from me, and it will never lead anywhere. I'm hardly an enviable party. As you know, my grandfather was a brewer, my family was dispossessed of what little land my father had managed to acquire before the invasion, and I have no fortune to compensate for that fact."

There was a silence and the body against her went unnaturally still. What was happening? What had she said? Slowly, she straightened her back to look at Cameron. Gone was the teasing in his eyes. He had never looked more serious—or more alluring.

"You *do* have a fortune now. That's what I came to tell you."

It was her turn to still. Had she heard him right? She had a fortune? How? Had her brother given Cameron some money to be handed over to her once they had arrived in Scotland? It seemed unlikely, as he had little to spare, but it was the only explanation she could think of.

The silence stretched, quicky becoming unbearable.

Cameron stood up and started to pace around the chapel, evidently trying to find the best way to word his explanation. In the end Bethan lost patience and planted herself in front of him. The master of bluntness was choosing this moment for being circumspect? Well, she would not stand for it.

"Speak, damn you!" she hissed. "You can't expect me to wait patiently after what you just said!"

He gave a sigh and shook his head. "I had forgotten what

unsuitable language you had acquired at the tavern. So unladylike."

"You know I'm not truly a lady, you've said it enough times," was her curt retort. For once she was not in the mood to tease him. "And believe me, you have heard nothing. Do not force me to say more."

"Heaven forbid that I should. We are in a chapel, in case you hadn't noticed."

The light in his eyes, however, seemed to suggest he would like nothing more than to hear what she was capable of. But Bethan didn't indulge him. He'd just made the most shocking revelation, and she needed to hear more. His face lost all trace of amusement, and she knew that was finally about to answer her question.

"Listen. I was not aware of this, as I was already on my way to Wales by then, but about a month ago Dougal was rewarded by the Bruce for his loyalty to him. It seems his involvement was of crucial importance in several of the sieges they've laid over the years. Added to the estates he holds from my brother, it makes for a considerable fortune. And, when he lay dying from the bloody flux that killed him, knowing he was not going to make it, he bequeathed it all to you."

"To...?"

"To you," Cameron confirmed, his gaze unwavering.

Thunder fell at Bethan's feet. "But why?"

"Dougal was not without honor, and he knew this union had been arranged to ensure your future." He shrugged. "I imagine he thought to use that as compensation for having failed to make you Lady Cambell and leaving you in a difficult situation."

Yes... But if what she had heard was true, her situation was not as dire as she had first imagined. She was now a rich woman, by all accounts.

"Are you sure?" She could barely believe it.

Cameron gave a rueful smile. "Aye, I've seen the papers, it's official. But don't rejoice too fast. Unfortunately, your problems are not over."

"What do you mean?"

"It seems that Dougal made no mystery of his intentions regarding his will and the news of your new fortune has spread fast. Master McDuff tells me that a number of local lairds of all ages and importance were seen lurking around Crois Dhubh in the last two weeks, biding their time like the vultures they are while Dougal lay abed."

"That's awful!" Bethan was appalled. How the men thought she would even consider marrying anyone who showed such cynicism was beyond her.

"Some asked to pay their respects to you yesterday after the funeral but were told you were resting. Most pretended to understand, but one was rather insistent. I need not tell you that your reputation as an extraordinarily beautiful woman, however old you may think you are, is only adding to your appeal." The corner of his mouth curled up. "So, it seems that you will have to fend potential suitors off rather than try to lure them in."

Well.

Bethan stared at her feet, speechless. What a spectacular reversal of fortune. She was a rich woman and free from a marriage she had never desired. Even more importantly, she was now in a position to marry whomever she chose—and apparently, candidates were already tripping over themselves to get to her. It was a lot to take in.

"I will need some time to think," she murmured.

"Of course." Cameron stood up. "Take all the time you need."

A moment later, she was alone in the chapel.

It did not take Bethan long to see that Cameron had been right about her problems having just started. The next day, no fewer than three visitors came sniffing about, two of which were old enough to be her father and rather rough-looking. The youngest one had been so bold that she had barely noticed his fair countenance. At least the two oldest ones had been respectful.

But Donald McDonald—the name alone would have been enough to disqualify him had she been of a mind to take his pursuit seriously—had found himself alone with her when master McDuff had unexpectedly been called away shortly after bringing him to her. It hadn't taken the man long to launch himself into an impassioned speech about her radiant beauty. When she'd told him she had no intention to think about marriage so soon after Dougal's demise, he had simply pounced on her. She wasn't sure what he'd hoped to achieve by raping her—compromise a woman he assumed to be a virgin so that she had no choice but to marry him or simply punish her for refusing him—but for a short but very real moment she had been scared out of her wits.

This had been a real assault, nothing like the misunderstanding at the tavern. McDonald had known who she was all along, and his intent had been crystal clear. There had been no bawdy jests, no entreaties. He had simply thrown her to the ground and lain on top of her, ready to take his pleasure.

"No!"

"Aye."

And with that word, he'd kissed her. Dear Lord, how was she to get out of this? He was far too strong and determined for her to hope stopping him.

In the end it was Murdo who came to her rescue.

He must have heard the cry of protest she'd made before

McDonald had crushed his mouth on hers because he burst into the solar, intent written all over his rugged face. He already knew what he would find in the room.

What was probably a frightful curse left his lips right before he grabbed the younger man by the arm and throat. A moment later, Bethan was free. Pinning her attacker to the wall as if he weighed no more than a child, Murdo unleashed his fury on to him. Bethan wasn't sure the man would survive if she did not intervene so she scrambled back to her feet as best she could and stumbled to the wall.

"Leave him. Please." She would not have anyone killed on her account, no matter how vile they were.

"Give me one good reason not to strangle him."

For more safety, she gave him two. "You stopped him in time. And I don't want trouble between your two clans."

"Aye, well, *he* should have thought of that before he attacked you."

"Please." To her horror, she was feeling her resolve waver. Why shouldn't Murdo strangle the man? Why did he deserve to be shown mercy when he'd ignored her protests, made the most of the fact that he happened to be the stronger of the two to rape her? What had happened had not happened by accident. Her attacker had meant to pounce, to take her, to hurt her. Why should he not be punished? No one had forced him to assault her, and she had made her feelings clear.

As if he'd sensed her hesitation and wanted to spare her a decision she would only regret later, Murdo released the McDonald laird. "God knows why the lady would want to spare your sorry hide, but you had better make sure you and I don't cross paths ever again, you piece of shite."

With those words, he threw him down the stairs head first. Bethan cried out in horror. How was the man supposed to survive such a fall? Surely a lifeless corpse would be the only thing Master McDuff would find. But a moment later she saw the McDonald hobble back to the horse tethered in the bailey down below. He was not dead, even if he might be bruised all over. Still trembling from shock at what had happened, or rather what could have happened, she slid onto the stone bench, as limp as water-logged seaweed.

This had been the most horrifying attack, and she was lucky to have escaped unscathed. As was her attacker.

"Thank you, Murdo. I don't know what I would have done without you."

He nodded briefly. "That's quite all right. The bastard had it coming. I've never been able to stand him. Are you all right, my lady?"

Bethan gave him a wan smile. No matter how many times Cameron and herself told the men she had no right to the title, they persisted in calling her "my lady." It never failed to amuse her. To think they had refused to believe her when she had claimed to be a lady that night at the tavern... It now seemed a decade ago. Since then, she had come to see that the men in the retinue were as good as Cameron had promised her. It did not surprise her, as he would never surround himself with scoundrels.

"I'm all right, thank you." She paused. "With your permission, though, we will not tell the laird what happened."

For a while it looked as if Murdo would argue. Then he let out a sigh. "Aye, you're right, since he's likely to kill the man for the offense."

Bethan recoiled. Would he really do such a thing as kill a man in cold blood? As Murdo had seen the attack, his heated reaction might be explained, but if Cameron did anything against Donald McDonald now, it would be nothing less than murder. Surely he wouldn't go to such lengths? The risk of him killing a man had not been the reason she wanted the secret kept. Rather, she felt foolish for not having been able to prevent the assault, and she thought Cameron had done enough for her already. Still, she nodded, deciding it was best not to tempt fate. Murdo wouldn't have spoken thus if he didn't think it a likely outcome. He knew his laird better than she did.

"Please, don't tell him."

"I won't. Here. Have a drink. It will help."

Bethan gratefully drank the ale he'd poured her. Once the cup was empty, she felt much better. When her gaze met Murdo's, the words she'd been trying to repress burst through her lips. "I swear I told him I did not want—"

He did not let her finish. "I have no doubt you did. But some men's brains and ears don't seem to function properly once their cocks—" He stopped and cleared his throat. "Begging your pardon, my lady. Once they've, erm, decided they want a woman."

Yes. While others would never force anyone, even a whore. This was the chance to put the incident outside the tavern at rest and establish once and for all that she had nothing to fear from Cameron's men. "What would you do if a woman you wanted to bed didn't want you?"

"I would make sure to double my efforts at seducing her." He winked, as if to indicate he did not doubt the result he would achieve.

"And if she still refused you?"

He scowled, glancing to the wall where a moment ago he had pinned McDonald. He thought she was talking about what had just happened. She wasn't. "Then I would see to my needs myself," he growled. "Pardon my crudeness again, but surely you must know that I would never take a woman who didn't want me?"

"Even if you were drunk?"

Another scowl. "I'm never that drunk."

"Even if she was a— Even if she was a w..." She didn't manage to say it, but Murdo understood.

"A whore is still a woman, free to choose, is she not? If she really didn't want me, or my coin, then I'd have no choice but to use my—" He stopped abruptly and frowned. "Wait. Why are you asking me all this?"

"No reason." Damn and blast, she had to stop this, or he would get suspicious. "I guess I needed to see not all men would behave like McDonald just did."

His face tightened. "You can be assured of it. I'm telling you true, my lady, only despicable weasels would attack a woman thus. And I'm not a weasel."

"No, you're not. Well, thank you."

Tears started to sting her eyes as soon as Murdo closed the door behind him. Was this what her life would be from now on? Would she have to fend off attacks from men who wanted to possess her, in order to get to her new fortune? What a frightful prospect that was.

Bethan stayed in the solar, staring through the window until it was too dark to see anything.

Chapter Nine

"I will have to leave," Bethan announced the following morning.

Everyone had broken their fast in the hall with bowls of creamy porridge. In just a few days, this new Scottish dish had become a favorite of hers and she already knew this was what she would want to eat in the morning for the rest of her life. She would have to make sure to ask the cook for the method before setting off, since no one in Wales had heard of it.

"Leave?" Cameron placed his spoon down.

"Yes. There is nothing here for me except trouble."

"Surely it can wait a few days? You've been on the road almost a month already, you'll need a rest."

Yes, a rest would have been nice, but she didn't have that luxury. McDonald's attack was proof enough. Who would be the next man to think he could use her body to build his fortune? But since she had decided to keep the events of the previous day a secret, she couldn't reveal the reason behind her decision to leave as soon as possible, so she stayed silent.

"Where will you go?" Cameron asked when he saw she wasn't going to answer.

In truth, she had no idea. Could she return to Castell Esgyrn? She was certain the Hunters would welcome her again, but she knew she would feel like a failure, coming back still unmarried, even if Dougal's defection was hardly her fault. Could she go live with Siaspar at Castell y Ddraig? As a thank you for her brother's hospitality, she could offer to look after his estate. Having no wife, mother, or sister with him, he might welcome the feminine touch, at least for a while, while she thought on a more permanent solution.

Bethan rubbed at her temple. This was a problem she could have done without. For years she had thought she would have a home here, in the Scottish Highlands, and she was even thinking she could come to like the country. On the way here, she had fallen under the charm of the rugged landscape. But with Dougal gone, she had no reason to stay at Crois Dhubh, and staying anywhere else in the vicinity, alone, put her at risk.

"I don't know yet. I will go to Wales and decide when I'm there." At least she had a few options, even if they were not ideal. The hand massaging her temple traveled to her neck and rubbed. God, she was so tired. "There is no rush."

"What is that?" she heard Cameron say.

"What is what?"

"This." Leaning over to her, he placed his finger, callused and warm, next to hers on the tender skin underneath her ear. Heat flooded through her. How he could make such a simple touch so sensual was mystery. "You have a scratch here."

A scratch? Courtesy of McDonald's attack, no doubt. The heat in her veins instantly turned to ice. She had hoped to keep the assault a secret from him and she'd thought to have succeeded.

"I must have caught myself with a pin this morning when I tried to put on a veil," she said in her best unconcerned voice.

"You're not wearing any veil," Cameron pointed out. "In fact, you never do."

Damn, of course he would have noticed she didn't. They had been together for a month. "I don't usually, but I wanted to wear one today. I changed my mind when I saw I could not pin it satisfactorily, probably because I'm out of practice."

"Mm." He didn't sound convinced.

The finger at her throat started to draw slow circles on her skin, stealing her sanity. She swallowed hard. Cameron must have felt it because he stood up abruptly, as if he'd only then realized what he was doing.

"Come. I need to show you the papers pertaining to your new fortune."

She nodded. The day before she had needed time to deal with the revelation, but she was now ready to see for herself how much her life had just changed. He led the way up to a room at the back of the solar Dougal had evidently used to write letters and conduct his affairs. It was small and sparsely furnished, rendering obvious the fact that the owner of the castle was barely ever home. It was a stark reminder of the kind of life she would have had if she'd married Dougal, one that sent shivers down her spine.

"Here. I will have this translated into English if you prefer, but as you can see, you are a rich woman."

Bethan stared at the piece of parchment Cameron had just laid flat on the table. The Gaelic was undecipherable, but the sums scattered here and there spoke for themselves. Indeed. She was now a rich woman. After having spent the best part of her life counting every coin, it was a bewildering discovery.

That still didn't tell her where to go or what to do, and it brought with it its own lot of problems. Her gaze wandered to the solar where the day before McDonald had assaulted her. Men would be after her. Only two days ago she had been worried no one would even think of proposing to her, now she knew some men would resort to rape to take her to the altar. Indeed, she had to leave, even if the thought of being parted from Cameron had her guts twisted in knots.

"Yes. I can see that. It only makes it imperative for me to leave as soon as possible." At home, no one would know about this new fortune of hers. She would be safe from men's machinations, free to choose her destiny. "Do you think one of your men would agree to escort me back to Wales?"

"One of my men?" Cameron sounded as if she'd just suggested he stabbed himself in the eye or something equally gruesome. "I will escort you myself, wherever you decide to go."

Her heart skipped a beat. He wanted to go with her? They weren't to say goodbye just yet? Relief spread through her, which was quickly replaced by something else. Something like excitement at the idea of being on the road alone with Cameron for days on end. She pretended to examine the piece of parchment to hide her turmoil.

"You've already spent almost two months away from your home and your clan," she murmured. "You're the laird. I cannot ask this of you."

"Come, Ealasaid," he growled. "Surely you know—"

She rounded on him. "What did you just call me?"

A corner of his mouth lifted. He'd seen her outrage and was enjoying it. The wretched man!

"Ealasaid. It's Elizabeth in Gaelic." Oh. Her anger deflated as quickly as it had come. Clearly, he had not meant to insult her, quite the contrary. In truth, she didn't know why she had reacted so hotly. She could only suppose all the events of the last few days had left her overwrought. "You did tell me that was what your name meant in Welsh?"

"Well, yes."

It was. So why did hearing the Gaelic version make her feel

so...so... What was she feeling, exactly? Damn and blast, discussions with Cameron Campbell made her whirl from one emotion to the next with dizzying speed.

"I don't need your escort." Suddenly she was certain being on the road alone with him for days on end was the last thing she should do.

"Well, you're getting it all the same."

"I cannot ask you to—"

"You're not asking, damn you! I'm offering. Are you going to gainsay everything I say?"

"What if I am? What are you going to do about it?"

"*Mo chreach!* You, my wee Welsh hellion, are too challenging by half. And far too tempting." He let his gaze wander all over her in the most shameful way. Irritation had been replaced by something altogether more worrying, something hot and fierce. "It is time I did something about *that.*"

His intention was only too clear. He was going to do what had seemed inevitable since they had set eyes on each other. Now that he knew she was no virgin, now that she was not betrothed anymore, nothing stood in their way; they could finally surrender to the desire burning between them. Bethan's whole body caught alight at the thought. This was what she wanted, what she was desperate for.

His mouth was on hers before she could beg him to kiss her, betraying a need as intense as hers. The kiss was fierce, almost too rough, and yet still not passionate enough. She could taste his lingering doubts as well as his desire for her, feel his body warring with his reason. No, not now! He could not hesitate now, when she was finally where she wanted to be, in his arms. He drew back, eyes ablaze, and she caught him by the tunic to prevent him from leaving.

"Cameron, please. More."

Every nerve ending ignited the moment his lips landed on

her throat, just under her ear. There was the gentlest of bites, followed by the naughtiest of licks. This was what she wanted, raw, unfettered desire. Everything within her relaxed, then tensed. There would be no holding back from now. She had kept her urges for this man in check from the moment she had met him, she had ridden next to him day after day and she had witnessed the proof of his desire for her on many occasions, she had been driven to the edge of madness imagining all they could do together at night. For weeks all she'd been able to think about was the touch of his lips and hands all over her body.

Now it was time to experience the real thing.

Bethan took his head between her hands and kissed him with all the passion she was capable of. In that moment they were fused as one. It was perfect already. And soon it would be even better, he would be inside her, like another part of her, and they would *be* one.

Still kissing her, Cameron pushed her back until she was leaning against the wall. The urgency of the move made her legs grow weak, made her desperate for more. As if he'd heard her silent plea, his mouth left her lips and moved back to her throat, sliding lower than before, all the way to the swell of her breasts in a heated trail. As if by sorcery, the edge of her bodice slid down, revealing her nipples.

"Fuck," she heard Cameron say between his teeth. That one, crude word and the urgency in his voice were enough to cause her insides to ripple.

A heartbeat later, his mouth, hot and demanding, started suckling her, his tongue exerting the perfect amount of pressure on her nipple. Her thoughts exploded into a million pieces. This was exquisite, and yet not enough. A strangled cry, almost a mewl, split the air. Hers, probably. She didn't know.

She was out of her mind with need.

A hand whipped under her skirts, and light fingers started to dance against the flesh of her inner thigh, sending goosebumps all over her body. Authoritatively, Cameron parted her legs with his knee, acting as if he had every right to do so and more. And oh, he did, because he was acting exactly as she wanted him to, doing exactly what she needed him to do. How arousing to feel that she was making him lose his mind with the need to possess her. Warmth spread through her when he covered her folds with his palm.

Yes! Touch me, right here, where I ache, she almost screamed.

"Christ, Ealasaid," he grunted against her wet nipple. "You would make me forget everything, do you know that? You make me mad."

He could equally have meant mad with anger or mad with lust, but Bethan didn't have time to wonder which one it was. His lips closed around her left nipple, and he resumed his sensual suckling. Slowly, as if to give her the opportunity to refuse, he slid one finger inside her and she thought she was going to pass out with the pleasure of it. She was pinned against the wall, utterly at his mercy and breathless with anticipation.

Surely by now he would have felt that he was driving her mad as well. Mad with lust. His thumb started stroking her gently, circling her intimate bud, drawing even more wetness from her grateful body, the movement a perfect match for the swirl of his tongue on her nipple. It was just as she'd imagined being in his arms would be. No, it was better, it was heaven. Cameron Campbell was the most self-assured, virile man she had ever been with, and she could already tell this lovemaking would be explosive. None of her other lovers had made her crave their touch thus.

"Yeeees..."

"Aye, you like that, sweetheart?" He carried on his intimate caress while the finger inside her kept teasing her. "Then how about this?"

Another finger joined the first, sliding in with disconcerting ease. The moves became faster and more precise, building the need inside her body to an almost unbearable pitch, heating her all the way to her toes. It was too much, and soon Bethan erupted in a riot of sensations, her body convulsing spasmodically around him. The idea that she was being pleasured in broad daylight against a wall only made her pleasure more intense and she bit the back of her hand to muffle the cries escaping her lips. Had it not been for Cameron's grip around her waist she would surely have collapsed. With her legs shaking uncontrollably, ready to give way from under her, she could hardly stand.

This had been as hot as hell, emotional, carnal, sweet, and everything in between.

Cameron was breathing as hard as if he'd just been sword training with three men at once.

Finally, he was doing what he'd been aching to do for weeks, and it was even better than he'd imagined. Bethan's sheath was gripping his fingers tight, sucking them in with the last of her spasms. They were coated with the proof of the pleasure he'd wrenched from her body. *He* had done that, he had given her what she needed, he had made her forget herself for one beautiful, perfect moment.

His self-control snapped at the thought. He'd wanted to take his time, make the most of what she had to offer, kiss her breasts until she writhed in ecstasy, sit her on the table and kneel between her legs to taste her deliciously soft flesh and then to let her pleasure him with her hands and mouth but it would not happen now. He was too taut with the need of having her, one kiss away from spilling his seed. Besides, the last thing he wanted was someone walking in on them and putting an end to the moment before he had been satisfied.

"My turn," he groaned, taking a step back.

There was no protest.

Cameron almost tore the laces from his braies, such was the haste with which he removed them, freeing a shaft that felt harder than the stone at his feet. He had no idea what it was about Bethan that set his loins on fire so, but he was on the verge of erupting like the youth he no longer was. Thank God she was no virgin, for he feared the knowledge he was about to take her innocence would not have been enough to stop him. He would have dishonored her—and himself—to finally have her. As it was, there was no need to worry about ruining or hurting her. The only thing he would focus on was giving them both the pleasure they deserved.

Taking himself in hand, he lifted one of her thighs, holding it in place around his waist. She was the perfect height for him, as if they'd been created to fit together, and wet against the tip of his cock, the most irresistible invitation a man could receive. Unable to wait any longer, he rammed into her to the hilt. There was a sharp intake of breath and a whimper. Immediately, he stilled.

"I'm sorry, lass, was that painful?" Damnation, his desire for her had turned him into a thoughtless brute, something he'd always been careful to avoid. Even if she was not a virgin, she did not deserve to be used thus.

"Painful? No," Bethan breathed in his ear, her voice different than usual, deeper, huskier. "That had to be the opposite of painful."

"Good." He nuzzled at her neck, making her moan in the way he loved. "Then let me start again."

She felt even better than in his dreams, hot and tight and slick. Cameron couldn't have stopped even if he'd wanted to, even if someone had walked into the room. He would simply have sent them to hell. Bethan clung to him and wrapped her other leg around his waist, letting him guide them both to ecstasy. The rhythm of his thrusts increased when she dug her nails in his shoulders, moaning what he imagined to be words of encouragement in Welsh. Soon her inner muscles flexed around him, and he was lost.

Cameron pushed one last time into her sweet softness and his whole body dissolved with the intensity of his pleasure. He placed one hand on the wall for support, holding Bethan pinned under his weight. It took a moment for him to catch his breath. When he was finally able to open his eyes, he saw that she was watching him. A lazy smile was floating on her lips; a smile he could do nothing but kiss.

"Do you ever make love in a bed?" she asked while he held her close, their bodies pressed tight against each other, their breaths mingled, his shaft still buried deep inside her.

"Is that a complaint?"

"Hardly." No. Perhaps not. She appeared quite satisfied, and she *had* come twice. "Only..."

He knew what she was saying. None of the other men she had gone to had taken her standing against a wall in a wild frenzy of lust. He could have let jealousy overcome him at the thought of these other men, but he did not, because she was right. The encounter had been raw, wild, pure perfection. It had been between them, and he would not let anything, or anyone spoil it.

Gently, he withdrew from her and lowered her back down to the floor. He would have liked to stay nestled in her warmth a while longer, but he wasn't sure he would have the strength to hold her much longer and the last thing he wanted was to drop her when his arms gave way. His whole body had gone limp. Or... Perhaps not everything had.

Cameron looked down in amazement. God's teeth, he was still semi-hard, despite the force of his release and he wanted nothing more than to take Bethan to the nearest bed and show her that he had no problem making love on a soft mattress or anywhere else.

"I make love wherever I need to, Ealasaid. Against the wall, on a table, in the forest if the mood takes me," he said, skimming her jaw with featherlight kisses. "But I will come to your bed tonight."

A single word, hardly more than a breath. "Tonight?"

"Tonight," he confirmed, tucking his rapidly hardening cock into his braies. Damnation, it wanted more. And so did he. After a month lusting after her, he was not going to be sated with one hurried spend. "This, exquisite as it was, has not satisfied me by a long shot. So be ready. I'm not finished with you yet."

Chapter Ten

Well, Cameron Campbell did indeed make love in a bed—and left his partner bewildered by the onslaught.

Bethan lay on her side, naked, warm and more content than she had ever been. The interlude in the room by the solar that morning had been explosive, but this lovemaking had been her every dream come true. Slow and gentle, hard and fast, hot and wild, and everything else she could think of, so much so that Cameron had fallen asleep almost as soon as he had rolled off her pulsing, sated body.

Though she was drowsy with an excess of pleasure herself, she could not fall asleep just yet. Instead, she watched him sleep in the moonlight, fighting the urge to caress his chest, with its smattering of copper-colored hairs, his arms, corded with lean muscles, his jaw where a dark ginger stubble had started to grow. So beautiful, so manly... She drank him in in one of his rare moments off guard. Not many people would have seen him in such a moment of abandon, only his mother when he was a child, and then the women he'd taken to bed later on in life. Had there been many? Probably. One didn't become so skilled in the art of pleasuring women without some practice. Besides, he looked too good not to attract attention, and he had no reason to resist temptation. Thank God she had not been an inexperienced virgin, and able to please him as much as he had pleased her.

He stirred a moment later, blinked as if trying to remember where he was, ran a hand though his tousled hair, then smiled when he saw her and it came back to him. Her heart melted at the same time as her core heated. How could anyone manage to look so adorable and virile at the same time? She had no idea.

"How long have I been asleep?" he rasped.

"Not long. It's still the middle of the night."

"Mm. Odd, I can't even remember falling asleep."

Bethan smiled. There was nothing odd about that, considering that after reaching his release in a storm of passion, he'd whispered that she'd killed him and then rolled off her in one heap, already half-asleep.

To her surprise, he took her hand and, interlacing his fingers with hers, brought it to his lips to kiss the inside of her palm. The gesture was incredibly tender. Did he behave thus with all his conquests she couldn't help but wonder? It mattered not, as long as he behaved like this with her, she decided, pushing the question out of her mind.

"Tell me. How do you choose your lovers?" She could tell the question had been on his mind since the moment she had admitted to not being a virgin and he thought that the intimacy they had shared that day allowed him to finally ask it. It did. "I know from your encounter with Sir Alan that you do not throw yourself at all the men who are interested in you."

"No." Her lips quivered. How she loved that he still wanted to tease her, even now that he had taken his pleasure. She would have hated to see him lose interest in her as a person after he'd possessed her body. "And I have not taken nearly as many men as you seem to think to my bed. It is not always easy to entice the ones I want."

"Come." Cameron scoffed. "You won't make me believe that for a moment. Any man in his right mind would give an arm to take you to bed."

"Not quite so. The first one I tried to seduce, my friend William, refused me on the grounds that he preferred men. There was a man who would have given an arm *not* to have to bed me. Besides, I'm hard to please," she added with a wave of the hand. "Most men repel me rather than attract me."

"Repel? Are the men in Wales that ugly?" Cameron smiled, stretching his long limbs with cat-like grace.

Bethan watched his muscles contract with the movement then stole a glance at his perfect profile. She smiled to herself. Compared to him, yes, most men seemed like pitiful imitations of manhood. She could not think of a single man who possessed half of Cameron Campbell's appeal. In any case, their appearance was not what had weighed the most in the balance when she had decided to refuse their offers.

"Most of the time, it was not their looks that was the problem. You would understand why I refused them if you had *heard* them. I had the distinct impression that all they were interested in was my beauty."

"I see." Cameron turned to his side, propping his head in his hand, the posture relaxed, the gleam in his eyes mocking. Like her, he was completely at ease with his nudity. "What else should they have been interested in? Your ability to swear better than they do? Your refusal to be cowed? Your willingness to discuss women riding their lovers and kneeling at their feet? Aye, there is much to like about you, Ealasaid, besides your beauty."

"And there is much to like about you," Bethan whispered, tracing her finger around Cameron's full, sensual lips. She had not known that such beauty could exist, or that it could affect you just to *look* at a man you desired.

"Who was the first man you took to your bed?"

Another woman might have taken exception to his question, but she did not. Betrothed women did not take lovers and surrender their maidenheads, nor did they tell other men about their love life. But she had done all this. Considering how open she had been with him, it was only fair that he should ask.

Besides, she was gratified to see that he was not so hypocritical as to pass judgment on her past affairs.

"I was seventeen when I shared my first kiss. I asked one of Castell Esgyrn's grooms to kiss me," she said, hiding her face in the crook of his neck. She had no idea what had made her confide this to him now. It was not what he'd asked.

Against her lips she felt the low rumble of a laugh. "So that was how it all started. Seventeen! Well. No wonder you're so accomplished in the art of pleasing a man."

Heat invaded her cheeks. This man really gave the most unusual compliments.

"It's not what you think," she explained hurriedly. "The three years since the signing of the marriage contract had just ended and I thought Dougal would arrive any day... I panicked, and went to the first boy I found, to give myself the illusion I had some say in what happened to me. In any case, it was a sweet, innocent kiss. I never asked him for more."

"Why didn't you?" Cameron pressed, drawing back to look at her in the eye. Bethan shook her head, refusing to answer his question.

A heartbeat later she found herself lying on her back, her wrists pinned on either side of her head, her body trapped under his much bigger one. The warmth, the weight of him was wonderful, the contact of his naked skin against her equally naked skin shocking, delicious. It made her think of all they had done earlier.

All she wanted to do now.

"Why, Ealasaid?" he repeated, eyes alight with amusement when she arched her back in supplication. "Why did you not ask the groom for more than a kiss?"

"I was young... I don't remember," she breathed. "Now let me go, you beast."

Or do what naked men do when they are lying in bed on top of a naked woman.

"The beast that I am will not be put off so easily." The kiss that followed this declaration was scorching and Bethan couldn't help a moan of protest when Cameron drew back. "Don't lie to me, you do remember why you did not press the boy for more, I can see it in your eyes. So tell me." He kissed the side of her throat, nuzzling against her as he did. "Why did you let him off?" Next his tongue swirled around the hollow at the base of her neck. "I should warn you that I am not going to let you go until you have answered my question. I've had a sleep, I could keep going all night."

Having issued his warning, he started to kiss her naked breast with deliberate thoroughness, leaving no place untouched, groaning all the while. Bethan let out a shaky laugh when he took the nipple in his mouth and sucked hard, as if to swallow it whole.

"If you mean to keep me under you and kiss me until I relent then I am not sure you have thought this through. I might just want to let you do just that. It is not exactly torture to be kissed thus, you know," she rasped.

There were no more threats, no more questions. "Tell me," was all he said before his mouth landed on her collarbone.

"No, this is not the way to convince me to talk." She smiled, pleasure warming her body. "It's too delicious, I don't want it to stop."

A moment later Bethan was not smiling anymore. She'd been wrong, the wretched man knew exactly what he was doing. The teasing, the slow kisses had utterly defeated her, made her desperate for more.

"Please, Cameron I can't take this anymore..." Instead of answering, he carried on with his maddening kisses, on her jaw, on her breasts, on her navel. "Are you going to make me beg?" she breathed, arching her back for what felt like the hundredth time.

"No, of course not, that would be cruel," he drawled, kissing the side of her hip. "Just tell me why you did not get into the boy's bed." He licked at her nipple before sucking it deep into his mouth. Again. Causing her to melt. Again.

"You know why," she gasped, driven to the edge of madness by the exquisite sensation.

"I think I do. Still, I'd like to be sure," he added, carrying on his ruthless teasing. Bethan let out a rasp. If he did not take her now, she would die.

"Because I thought he would not be the lover I wanted," she said hurriedly, keeping her eyes averted all the while. This confession felt even more intimate than what they had done earlier. "I knew from the start that I wanted someone more experienced, someone assured and bold."

Someone like you.

Cameron raised himself up on his elbows so he could hover over her and forced her to look at him. His eyes had gone liquid with desire, the color extraordinary, just like quicksilver.

"You wanted a man, not a boy, is that it?" he purred, allowing a smile to bloom on his lips. He'd known it all along, and he enjoyed making her say it.

"Yes. Now, I have answered your question," she said lightly. "I have held my end of the bargain; it is time you held yours."

"But of course. I am a man of my word."

With this promise, he lifted himself off her and made to leave the bed. The sudden loss of his weight and warmth was a shock.

"Wait, where are you going?" she shouted in dismay, catching his hand before he could stand up. Surely he was not leaving now?

"I said I would let you go when you had answered my question and you have, so I'm letting you go," he answered innocently. "Why, did you have something else in mind?"

The wretched, *wretched* man!

"I did." Pushing him back onto the mattress, Bethan came to lie on top of him. Seeing his eyes catch fire when she started to rub herself against his chest, she afforded a smile. He would pay for the torture he had just put her through. And then she would get her reward. "So, you like teasing, do you? Let us see how you handle it when the roles are reversed. Didn't you complain the other day that women never made you surrender to their will?"

"I did. Although you proved earlier that *you* weren't afraid to ride your lovers."

Yes. And he had loved it, as had she.

"Show me how much you love me taking charge," she whispered in his ear. "And if I like what you provoke in me, I might allow you to reach your release as well."

The faint scraping of metal against stone and hushed male voices.

It was only because he was still awake that Cameron heard them. His whole body tensed. There was no mistaking what was happening. Men, armed with swords, were coming up the staircase. Next to him, Bethan slept on, unaware of the danger. Thank God he'd had a sleep earlier or he would have been asleep himself right now, and unprepared for the intrusion.

Who was coming up to Bethan's chamber at this hour? As to why, he could guess only too well. No one paid visits at this hour, and in such a stealthy manner. The rich, beautiful Welshwoman who slept alone and unprotected was going to be abducted then raped and married off to one of the local lairds, not necessarily in that order. With the marriage already consummated, the man responsible for her ordeal would have no difficulty finding a priest who would agree to make the union legal. No one knew Bethan was not a virgin and her suitor would have thought the loss of her maidenhead would be enough to bind her to him.

Over his dead body.

Contrary to what the intruders were hoping, she was not alone, she was not unprotected. He was here, and with surprise on his side, he fully intended to emerge the victor from the confrontation. He could only congratulate himself for choosing this day to finally surrender to the desire he felt for Bethan. Had he not come to her bed, she would have been alone to face the attackers. There would have been no escaping them. She would have woken up and found herself pinned under her future husband, unable to fight him off. And on the morrow, Cameron would have found her gone, with no idea of what had happened to her.

It did not bear thinking about.

Silently, he left the bed, reached for the scabbard he had deposited on the chest earlier that evening and drew his sword out. There was no time to get dressed. For the first time in his life, he would have to fight naked. Armed, he flattened himself against the wall, ready for the attack he was sure to come.

A moment later the door opened without a creak. This was odd. Everyone could tell Crois Dhubh was in a bad state. Someone must have oiled the hinges earlier that day, in preparation for this moment, which meant not only that the attack had been premeditated, but also that the treacherous laird coming to abduct his rich bride had an accomplice within the castle. This was bad indeed, and questions would have to be asked in the morning. For now, he had to focus.

Cameron tightened his grip on the hilt of his sword and waited.

A shadow soon appeared in his line of vision, too dark for him to recognize who he was. Certain of the intruder's ill intent, he struck first. He could not afford to wait, since he had no idea how many men were coming, and he was alone and naked. If the man died from the blow, he would have only himself to blame. He should have thought better of coming to attack women in their beds.

Bethan was woken up by the cry of a man.

She bolted upright, staring ahead of her without discerning much. In the darkness, all she could see were shadows. But she could hear the terrible sound of steel hitting steel.

At the foot of the bed, three—or was it four?—men were locked in a sword fight, the tight space preventing them from using their weapons the way they were supposed to. Grunts and curses made clear this was no jest but a fight to the death. Why? What was happening? Who were these men? The only one she could identify, because he was the only one without clothes on, was Cameron. His pale skin glowed, making him appear almost unreal.

A hand landed on her ankle, bringing her back to the reality of the situation, and started to drag her to the edge of the bed. Without thinking, she flexed her leg and kicked with all her might. There was a scream when the man reeled backward.

Then someone struck him on the back of the head and everything went silent.

"Are you hurt?"

Cameron, thank God. He was alive, even if he sounded winded.

"No," she whispered, glancing at the shape crumpled on the floor. "He wanted to grab me, but I kicked him in the...in the..."

"No need to make the effort of finding a polite way of saying it. I understand. Good for you."

Cameron stood in front of her, a figure of power almost demonic in its aspect. Naked, with blood on his chest and a sword in his hand he presented such an image of violence that she took in a shaky breath. How odd to think that this formidable warrior had been in her bed not too long ago, stroking her with careful tenderness, then taking her with unbridled lust.

"What happened? Who are they?" she asked, looking at the three men lying on the floor. They were sprawled face down, but she doubted she would have recognized them even if they had been looking up to the ceiling.

"We'll soon find out."

With a kick, he turned over the one who had grabbed her ankle. At that moment, the moon appeared from behind the clouds, shedding enough light for them to identify the young laird who had assaulted her the other day. There was no mistaking his face, as she was certain it would haunt her nightmares for years to come. She recalled every line, every groove. The mole at the side of his nose, the flecks of brown in his hazel eyes. She even remembered the way he smelled.

"Donald McDonald, one of the local lairds," Cameron said, evidently thinking she didn't know the man and needed him to identify him. She didn't. Unfortunately.

She shivered, horrified at the man's determination to have

her. Having been stopped the other day, he had decided to come find her when no one could come to her aid. What would have happened had Cameron not been in her bed tonight didn't bear thinking about.

Why, oh, why had she stopped Murdo from killing her attacker? she thought savagely. He'd been given a chance to live, and less than two days later, he was back for more. He hadn't deserved her mercy.

Her gaze landed on Cameron, who was still panting hard after his confrontation with three men. She remembered thinking it would be arousing to see him fight to protect her from assault the evening they had met. Well, he had done just that, and her mind was irrevocably changed. It wasn't arousing, it was terrifying. Never again did she wish to see men fight and kill one another on her behalf.

With a growl, he retrieved her shift from the floor where it had landed earlier. "Get dressed, Ealasaid." He sheathed his sword before reaching for his own clothes. "We need to talk, and I will not risk the men coming to while are discussing what needs to be done next."

"You mean they are not dead?" She wouldn't have been surprised if he'd run them through with his sword. After all, he'd been on his own against three, his survival and her rescue would have justified every ruthlessness on his part.

He shrugged on his undershirt and braies, not bothering with the tunic. "One of them definitely is dead. But the other two could wake up any moment. I need you out of here and safe when they do."

Nodding, she donned her gown and walked over to the door, careful not to step over the men. Which one was the dead one? Bile rose in her throat at the idea that there was a corpse in the room with her.

Her legs less steady than she would have liked, she followed

Cameron to the great hall, where the men of his retinue were sleeping, curled up in a corner. The only one missing was McBain. He'd been sent home the moment they had arrived, which had not surprised her.

"Angus, Murdo!"

The men snapped to attention, while Cameron fired up orders in rapid Gaelic. Though Bethan did not understand more than the odd word, the gist was pretty obvious. Two of the men were sent up to her chamber to retrieve the corpse and neutralize the survivors, who would be questioned as soon as they came to. The others were sent to investigate how the McDonalds had entered the castle.

Once they were alone again, Cameron poured them both a cup of ale.

"This decrepit castle is too hard to defend properly. We leave at dawn," he decreed, emptying his own cup. "Assemble what you want to take with you now. The rest of your possessions can be sent later on. We'll go to Nead an Diabhail first, where we'll decide what to do next."

The instructions were given with brisk efficiency, just like before, in the room. But this time Bethan rebelled. He was allowing her no say in the matter, or even asking her opinion. Everything within her bristled.

"I'm not going to your castle," she answered. "I told you I wanted to go to Wales, so I might as well—"

He stopped her with a cutting gesture of the hand. "Keep your protests." He had never sounded more implacable or more determined. "I am taking you to my castle. I can defend you better there while we think. Then once we have come up with a plan, I am taking you to Wales, where I agree you will be safer. This is not a matter of debate. You are mine to protect."

"I am not. I never actually married your nephew; I am not a member of your family or even your clan." What was possessing her to be so contrary she had no idea, but she had just found out how powerless she was, and she hated it. At least in this she had some say. "You do not owe me anything."

The flash of fury in the gray eyes almost frightened her. "If you care for my sanity, you will never repeat such a claim. A woman betrothed to someone of my family, whether the wedding took place or not, will benefit from my protection until the day she dies. That is a question of honor and non negotiable." He took another step toward her, all brooding intensity. "As to women who have shared my bed, their welfare is most definitely my affair. Do not forget it again. Christ, Ealasaid, how can you even suppose that I would not want to keep you safe after what happened between us?"

Bethan did her best not to waver. He wanted to help, and in truth she needed him. She could not travel to Castell y Ddraig alone. It was too dangerous. He was right. They needed to think before they acted.

Her hand landed on his forearm, a gesture of surrender and thank you.

"Very well. I shall go and prepare."

Chapter Eleven

The contrast between Crois Dhubh and Cameron's home was glaring. As much as she had felt ill at ease in the draughty, grim castle buried at the bottom of the valley, she could actually see herself living here. Situated at the edge of a tranquil *loch*, surrounded by rolling hills carpeted with purple blooms that scented the air with their subtle sweetness, Nead an Diabhail was an idyllic place, despite the fearsome name. Indeed, the Devil had never set foot or even glanced this way, she was certain of it. But it would seem that she would not be allowed to spend more than a few days here. Soon, they would have to leave and get to a place of safety.

The day after their arrival, Murdo had ridden through the gate, his face like thunder, his horse half-dead from exhaustion. Cameron and Bethan, who happened to be in the bailey, hurried over to him.

"You were right to take her ladyship away," he said without preamble—and in English. Bethan was grateful to see he seemed to think she had the right to hear what he had to say.

"What happened?" Cameron snapped, running a soothing hand over the stallion's rump. The poor beast was panting hard, betraying the haste of his rider. Bethan placed her hand on his soft muzzle, trying to calm the beatings of her own heart. This would not be good, she could sense it.

"Moments after you left yesterday, Malcolm McDonald came, enquiring after his brother. Bold as you please, he said he knew something must have gone wrong because Donald didn't turn up at the meeting point with his Welsh bride during the night."

"Did he now?"

"Aye." The word was little more than a growl. Dear, oh, dear, the man was truly a grizzled bear when he wanted to be. "We...erm, asked him some questions, and he revealed the plan the McDonald brothers had hatched between themselves."

Murdo explained that the young laird, incensed at her refusal to marry him, and more determined than ever to replenish his clan's coffers by a match with a rich woman, had decided to force her hand by abducting her, a practice that was unfortunately not uncommon. Bethan had heard of many a rich and well-born woman being taken away and raped by men who wanted their fortunes for themselves. In her country, there was the famous case of Nest ferch Rhys, the daughter of the last king of Deheubarth, of course, but she was not the only one. Now it seemed that Dougal's generosity had placed her in danger of being the next victim of such a heinous plot.

"Aye. We already suspected that was what the bastard's intent had been," Cameron said, his hand going to the hilt of his sword, and she knew that he was remembering how the man had tried to grab her from her bed, naked and helpless. What he didn't know was that there had been another attempt at rape before that, in the solar.

Murdo glanced at her, clearly of the opinion that she should speak now. Bethan shook her head. Cameron was already on the verge of an outburst. She could not risk making things worse than they already were. In a few days she would be out of here, it was not worth the Campbells starting a feud with the McDonalds, or anyone, on her account.

"There's more," Murdo carried on. "I'm afraid the McDonald died from his injuries while we were talking with his brother. Only one of the three men was able to leave Crois Dhubh with Malcolm's retinue."

Bethan gasped in horror. Despite what he had done, she hadn't wanted the man dead. But the blow to the head he had received for grabbing her ankle seemed to have been fatal.

"He's dead you say?" Cameron didn't seem to share her consternation.

"Aye." Murdo didn't sound sorry either. "Malcolm swore revenge against you for killing him and has vowed he would marry the lady himself instead. They must really be desperate for coin. I'm certain he has no intention of wooing her ladyship, but rather do like his brother, and simply abduct her. Nevertheless, we had no choice but to let him go. Thus far he has done nothing wrong."

"Bloody hell, this is a right mess." Cameron snarled. "We had better leave for Wales without delay, and place Bethan out of reach of the people who know about her new fortune, which will be most of the Highlands by now."

"Aye," Murdo agreed. "We have to take her to safety, especially as we still don't know who let the bastards in the castle."

This time when the two men started to plan the trip to Wales Bethan did not utter a word of protest. She did need to leave; it was not safe for her to stay in those conditions. Too many people had died already. It was time it all came to an end.

That night, Morag, the serving girl Cameron had assigned to her because she spoke English, found her weeping in her bedchamber.

"Oh, my lady!" she cried out. Just like everyone else, she

simply refused to accept that Bethan did not have a claim to the title. Acting with surprising familiarity, she dropped the clothes she was carrying on the bed and drew nearer, concern etched on her face. "What on earth is the matter?"

What could Bethan say?

My life is a mess. I have no idea what to do or where to go. Men are ready to commit unspeakable crimes because I suddenly became a rich woman. Two people have died because of it. And I'm falling in love with a man I will likely never see again once this madness is all over.

In the end she focused on the least personal of the problems. What harm would it do to confide in the girl? She sensed she would find a sympathetic ear.

"I have to flee Scotland before I'm abducted by Malcolm McDonald. Though he doesn't know me, hasn't even seen me, he's intent on marrying me by force to replenish his family's coffers. His brother tried to do the same thing only the other day and ended up dead because of it."

"A man is so eager to marry you that he is ready to abduct you to have you?"

The girl's eyes were wide with awe. It seemed she thought this terribly romantic, which it most decidedly was not. He had no interest in her, but in her newly found fortune, and he was not even considering wooing her, which would have been the honorable thing to do, but raping her.

"You know..." Morag carried on when she stayed silent. "You could do a lot worse than Malcolm McDonald, if I may say so. With his brother dead, he will likely be the next laird, a most enviable position. I saw him once, two years ago, at a gathering. He's young, strong, and easy on the eye."

So what if he was? Bethan blinked. "Did you hear me, Morag? He's a scoundrel who is not above forcing his attentions on unwilling women in order to trap them into marriage. I think I could do a lot better than that."

"Yes, of course, you're so beautiful! And now that you are a lady of means, you could have anyone." Still, the light in the girl's eyes remained bright. Apparently, young Malcolm had made quite an impression on her. "You are certain you won't regret your decision? The woman who becomes Laird McDonald's wife will have a good life."

"Very certain." She would not marry another man who had been imposed on her, one who used rape and abduction as means of coercion. "In any case, I shall leave soon. Laird Campbell and his men are this moment deciding on the best way forward. I wouldn't be surprised if Malcolm McDonald was lying in ambush somewhere. The more we wait, the more time he will have to get organized."

What would the Campbells decide? Would they try to slip unnoticed under his nose, or brazen it out, and travel with such a retinue that her enemy would have no chance of getting near her? Probably the first option. She doubted Cameron would want to take so many men away from his land at the same time, especially when he was leaving himself.

"I will accompany you to Wales," Morag suddenly announced. "'Tis not right that you should travel in the company of rough men without even a maid to help you. And look, your clothes have just arrived from Crois Dhubh. We can take the most precious ones along with us." She nodded toward the dresses she had deposited on the bed earlier.

Bethan barely repressed a scowl. What was the woman thinking? They would be riding hard to escape capture, not going on a pleasure outing. The precious dresses would have to be sent later on. In any case, what happened to her clothes was the least of her worries. "This will be dangerous. We'll be fleeing for our lives. I cannot in all conscience ask you to place yourself at risk."

"Begging your pardon, my lady, but this will be an adventure like no other for me. I have never been anywhere other than Nead an Diabhail or done anything other than toil in the kitchen. I would like a chance to better myself, see the world, and this might be it."

There was such hope in the girl's eyes that Bethan felt her irritation melt away. How could she refuse her this chance to live a little? But it was not her decision to make. She would not be the one responsible for the safety of not one, but two women while on the road. Wouldn't having Morag with them complicate matters further for Cameron?

She sighed. "Very well. I will speak to Laird Campbell, but I can't vouch for his answer."

"Thank you, my lady! I promise you won't regret it."

Bethan went to bed more anxious than ever. In the morning, Cameron announced that they would leave the following day at dawn. Murdo had ridden back to Crois Dhubh to get Angus, who would ride with them to Castell y Ddraig. The two of them would be back this evening, in time to rest before departing.

"Morag wants to come with us to Wales," she told him, remembering her promise to the girl. "She says she wants to help."

"Does she?"

Cameron was surprised. His men, Angus in particular, had many a time complained that the girl was lazy and selfish, and from what little he had seen, he tended to agree. That she would want to place herself in danger to help someone she didn't know made no sense. His first impulse was to refuse but then he thought better of it. Perhaps it wasn't such a bad idea after all. He'd been racking his brain for a way to get past McDonald's men, who, he was certain, were waiting to intercept them on the road south. The girl's unexpected request had just provided him with a solution.

"That could actually work to our advantage," he said slowly. "Malcolm McDonald has never met you."

"No, only his brother has," Bethan confirmed in a low voice. For a moment he wondered what had caused her to flush, but then he remembered how the man had tried to grab her while she lay naked in bed and how she had been forced to defend herself. Cameron pushed the disturbing image from his mind to focus on the problem at hand.

"Morag is young, she has brown hair, and so could pass for you from a distance," he carried on. The more he thought about it, the more this seemed like a good plan. "We will have her ride with the two men as if she were you. The two of us will follow discreetly while they lead the way. McDonald no doubt expects me to have sent men with you, rather than go myself, so he will not be suspicious when he sees only Murdo and Angus ride past. He will stop the three of them instead of you, his true target."

"No, 'tis too dangerous," Bethan said immediately. Apparently, even if she understood that this might be the answer to their problem, she was loath to expose the girl. He understood her scruples, but he was certain this could work.

"There will be no real danger," he argued, sure of himself. "Morag will easily convince him she's not the Welsh bride he seeks by talking to him in Gaelic. The men will be along to defend her if anything happens. In any case, the deception need not last long, just enough time for us to ride past unnoticed. By the time McDonald has realized his mistake, we'll be long gone."

The risk was minimal. He would not have exposed Morag or anyone else willingly, but the girl had volunteered, so he would make the most of the opportunity and be sure to reward her once they were back home safely. She had everything to gain from helping them, and very little to lose. At worst, McDonald would frighten her by his intensity but as Angus and Murdo would be with her, and the deception only needed to last long enough for them to slip past, she would quickly recover.

"If you say so." Bethan still sounded dubious.

His body moved before he'd decided to draw her into his arms. "Aye, I'm sure. And worry not, I will not let anything happen to her—or you."

This time it was his mouth which acted of its own accord. It landed on Bethan's lips in a soft kiss, a kiss that made his heart flutter but did not reach his groin. Odd. Since when did he not get hard while kissing beautiful women? Since now, apparently. And the strangest thing of all, he didn't feel as if anything was missing. He straightened up, keeping her tight against him.

"Why did you do that?" she asked, sounding breathless despite the innocence of the kiss.

It made him smile. She had not questioned his actions when he had pinned her against the wall behind the solar or positioned her on her hands and knees in her bed later that night, as if he had every right in acting so authoritatively with her. And yet she was wondering about this chaste, little kiss. It was as if she didn't understand why he would want to kiss her in tenderness, when it would lead to nothing else. He wasn't sure he quite understood either, so he didn't answer.

"If you'll forgive me, I have a few matters to attend to before we leave."

It was not ideal for him to leave so soon after having come back from a lengthy trip to Wales, but Cameron could not see any other way.

For better or for worse, he was now responsible for Bethan.

Chapter Twelve

The following morning, they set off at dawn, as arranged. Morag, who had been wrapped in a hooded cloak, led the way alongside Angus and Murdo, while Cameron and Bethan followed at a small distance.

At first everything went according to plan. But, as they progressed, Cameron started to wonder at his men's behavior. Angus and Murdo were stopping far more often than necessary. What was going on? Perhaps Morag, unused to riding, was the one urging them to a halt, but he doubted it. Every time the three of them stopped, the men were the only ones disappearing into the bushes, while she remained in the saddle, waiting patiently. And when they rode on, they sat stooped and limp, looking nothing like the proud warriors he knew them to be.

Something was definitely wrong.

"Next time they stop, we'll join them and ask them what the matter is," he told Bethan, even if by now he had a fair idea of what that might be. The two of them had the flux.

What rotten luck. They needed to be on high alert in case McDonald jumped, but they could not be as reliable as usual with their bowels roiling. One of them being incapacitated would have been bad enough, but both? Should the whole company turn back, and wait until the two men got better before setting off again? This first leg of the journey, so close to home, was the perilous part, the moment when he needed Murdo and Angus at their best, not rushing to the bushes at every opportunity, leaving Morag alone and vulnerable to attack.

Soon, there was another halt. Cameron signaled to Bethan that they should cut through the woods to get nearer to the three riders. Just as they'd dismounted and he was about to reveal their presence to the men, a war cry split the air. Before he knew what he was doing, he'd shoved Bethan down to the ground and covered her with his body. A loose arrow was an all too real possibility.

Mayhem erupted into the clearing as a dozen men jumped out of their hiding places to surround Morag, who'd once again been left on her own.

Damn and blast! Cameron had not imagined McDonald would have assembled such a large force in such a short time. He must be desperate for Bethan's fortune indeed. Murdo, who'd disappeared into the bushes a moment ago, was brought back into the clearing, bound and gagged, before being thrown to the ground. Angus tried to put up a fight despite his pallor, but he was equally subdued and placed next to his helpless friend.

Though his blood was boiling, Cameron had no choice but to remain where he was. Bethan could not be seen right now, that was the whole point of the deception. Besides, what could he do alone against twelve men? His two friends had not been killed, that was the main thing. Now McDonald would see his mistake and leave. And yet... Doubt assaulted him. Would the bastard not use Morag to ease his frustration when he found out he'd been duped? It was all too possible, as she was now on her own and defenseless.

It was clear from the panicked look Bethan threw him that she was thinking the same thing. She would resent him for refusing to heed her warning and placing an innocent woman in danger and wanted him to go the girl's rescue. Though he shared her anguish, he shook his head. There was nothing he could do for now, save hope that McDonald was only after coin, and would leave when he saw he would never get it by abducting a servant.

Heart thumping hard, he waited and then saw a man emerge from behind the riders.

"Malcolm," he breathed into Bethan's ear, even though she would have guessed the man's identity.

"Yes," she breathed back.

With dark hair and sparkling hazel eyes, the new McDonald laird was handsome enough, she supposed, but Bethan could not help a shiver. He looked exactly like his brother, in other words, like a man who had almost raped her. It was enough to make him abhorrent to her.

Morag, to her credit, did not seem to panic, even when Malcolm gave her a smile that could only have been described as sinister.

"Bethan ferch Morgan. I am Malcolm McDonald, chief of the McDonald clan. You refused my brother, but you will be my wife," he said in English, satisfaction evident in his voice. "Before tonight you and I will be wedded and bedded. The priest is waiting for us in the kirk yonder. There will be no escaping this time."

A silence, then a question, clearly audible in the stillness of the clearing.

"Who's to say I want to escape?"

With those words Morag threw off her cloak and revealed a

blue gown that could not belong to a servant. A gown Bethan recognized. Her mouth opened in shock. She'd had no idea that the woman had dressed in one of her dresses for the trip. Why? What was she doing?

And then she understood.

Morag was sacrificing herself to buy her time and allow her to escape. That was why she was not panicking, why she had made sure to wear a dress that hid her real identity, why she was drawing out the pretense for as long as possible. *I promise you won't regret it*, she'd told her the night she had asked to join the retinue.

Bethan's stomach gave a lurch. She could not let her do this. It was too dangerous. Malcolm was bent on rape, which was bad enough. But he might well kill her in a fit of rage when he understood that his plans had been thwarted.

"N—"

Cameron's hand clamped on her mouth before she could utter the word.

"Hush," he growled in her ear. He was still lying protectively on top of her after having thrown her to the ground earlier. "You are safe here, hidden from view. I will not let you be captured now."

But couldn't he see? They had to help the girl before it was too late! Angus and Murdo were writhing furiously, evidently in agreement with her. But with their mouths gagged they could not talk and expose the lie. Bethan tried to fight Cameron's hold. In vain. The arm around her waist was iron-hard, the hand holding her mouth shut, unrelenting. She could barely move, even if her breathing was unimpaired. Still, she moaned in protest. He had to let her go; they could not leave Morag in such a predicament alone. She would never forgive herself if anything happened to the girl. How could Cameron be so heartless?

"Do you want me to knock you senseless? I will do it if it stops you from placing yourself in danger," he warned, speaking low in her ear. She stopped fighting, believing he would not hesitate. "I will not release you until you have listened to me. Think! There is something amiss here. Why is Morag wearing a velvet gown? Were you the one suggesting she dressed thus?" She shook her head. That the girl had put one of her dresses on had come as a surprise to her as well. "Did you ask her to pretend to be you in case we were put upon?" Again, a denial. "Who prepared the food for Angus and Murdo this morning? The food that evidently made them sick?"

Bethan stilled.

Morag.

Morag had been the one preparing the food and ale. Morag had insisted she be part of the escort. She had made no mystery of what she thought of Malcolm McDonald. She had asked Bethan if she was sure she didn't want the man. It all became clear. The girl had meant to usurp her place all along, make the most of the McDonald laird's desperation to marry to trap the man she desired into a union with her.

She had said she wanted to better herself. This was the solution she had found.

Bethan didn't know whether to be appalled or impressed. She lifted her gaze to Cameron and nodded to indicate she had understood what he was trying to tell her and would not protest anymore. He took his hand away, stroking her cheek lightly as he did, a mark of approval.

"This is not just a distraction. She is not going to reveal her identity until they are married," she told him in a breath. The girl had not so much wanted to help her as to give herself a chance at a more prestigious life.

"Aye," Cameron confirmed, sliding off of her at last. "I think she saw an opportunity, that's why she asked to accompany you to Wales. She hoped that Malcolm would indeed stop us on the road, would mistake her for you if she looked like a rich lady and would marry her before he realized his mistake, binding him to her permanently. She made sure Angus and Murdo were in no state to fight, so as to ensure she did fall into the McDonalds' hands. How did I not guess something was amiss? Though I did think it awfully unlucky that both of them should be struck by the illness at the same time..."

"So did I. And now, with their mouths gagged, they won't be able to go against what she says." It was perfect. Had Morag not been escorted by fierce warriors who were doing their best to defend her, McDonald might have suspected a trap. As it was, he had no reason to be suspicious. The two Scots looked suitably furious at their powerlessness.

Cameron rubbed his jaw pensively. "'Tis a foolish and dangerous plan if you ask me. The bastard might well marry her, since he has no reason to suspect she is not who she claims she is, but it will not take him long to understand that she is not the rich woman he wanted. And then what does she think he'll do?"

Indeed. She would be lucky to get away with her life. Bile rose in Bethan's throat. She could not let this happen. "Angus and Murdo might be incapacitated, but we are not. We cannot let her get away with the deception. Please. You know what he means to do to, we must—"

Before she could finish her sentence Morag lifted the hem of her gown to reveal a shapely leg. Being on a horse helped her to display it to its advantage and appreciative grunts were heard from the men.

"We could always be bedded now, my laird," she said with an engaging smile. "It would save us some time later. I refused your brother because the fool tried to woo me, even though I knew he was only after my money. But I can tell you want me, enough to fight for me, and I like a man who knows what he wants and is not afraid to take it." The hem of the gown went up another inch. "Show me you're not a weak fool. Show me just how much you want me."

Bethan blinked. No. Surely the girl didn't mean to— Not here? Not like that?

"She's not going to—"

Cameron let out a growl. "She is. The sly minx means to ensure that the marriage is indissoluble, or at least to make it as difficult as possible for McDonald to annul it when he discovers the truth. I cannot say I feel sorry for him, considering the length he was prepared to go to to coerce you into a match with him. He will be given a taste of his own medicine and find himself married to a woman who is of no use to him."

She would have been happy to see him punished too, but unfortunately, it was not that simple. "But Morag..." What would happen to her when Malcolm found out he'd been tricked? He was hardly going to forgive the humiliation or accept that he was married to a mere servant. Would he kill her when annulment proved impossible? She would put nothing past the man.

"Fret not. She will have weighed the risks carefully. If she acquits herself well of the task of pleasing him, he might agree to keep her as a mistress." Bethan's mouth fell open. Was this supposed to reassure her? Cameron made a helpless gesture. "Aye, I ken it, but you can see how it is. She's hardly being forced into anything. Angus did warn me she was lazy and self-ish. If she wants to ensure herself a different life than that of a servant by beating McDonald at his own game, then she's welcome to it. She's offered us the best chance for escape we could have hoped for."

"I suppose." Cameron was right. Judging from what they were seeing, Morag was hardly being raped.

"I assume that she is a virgin and will use the loss of her maidenhead to prove that the union was indeed consummated. Little does she know that the woman she is impersonating is not as innocent as she is."

Bethan reddened. No, she was not an innocent maiden, he knew it firsthand.

She turned her attention back to the clearing. While they'd been talking Malcolm had helped Morag down from the saddle. His intention to take her up on her bold offer was written all over his face. His eyes were glowing with lust.

"I will send my men away if you prefer," he told his bride-to-be with a smile that sent bile to Bethan's throat. He was making it sound as if he were being chivalrous. "Or we could use them as witnesses that our union was indeed consummated."

Far from being outraged, Morag agreed to this suggestion which served her purpose as well. She laughed, and Bethan saw that she was not in the least nervous—or appalled at the idea of being taken under the eyes of a dozen men. It would seem that she was utterly under Malcolm McDonald's spell and ready to do anything to have him.

"It's not a problem to have them watch," she said coyly. "As long as you don't ask them to join us."

"I won't." The man unbuckled his scabbard without further ado. "There will be no need to. I know what to do and will not leave you wanting. By the Virgin, Lady Bethan, but you are bold! I had heard tales of your beauty, and you are certainly pleasing to the eye," he added with an appreciative tilt of the head. "But you are also as bold as the most seasoned whore."

"I am not a whore!" Bethan hissed between her teeth.

"I know you're not, Ealasaid," Cameron purred in her ear. "But Morag certainly is, and McDonald is convinced that she is you."

Yes, considering the way the serving girl was acting, it was no wonder the man thought her bold. Bethan felt her whole body sag in defeat. There was nothing else to do here. Morag had made her decision; she would have to face the consequences. And with luck, Angus and Murdo would be released when the retinue left for the kirk.

"Please, let us leave while they..." She glanced at the couple who were now on the ground, tearing at each other's clothes. This was definitely not a rape, Morag was just as eager as her abductor to consummate this union. The men in the clearing let out lecherous grunts when one of her breasts was revealed. "While they are busy," she finished, averting her gaze. This was sickening.

"An excellent idea."

Cameron silently led her back to the horses. A moment later they were galloping away on the south road, confident no one was after them.

"I guess I should be grateful to Morag for making the task of saving you from Malcolm McDonald a lot easier than I had anticipated," he said when they slowed down to a trot to allow the horses to breathe.

Yes, Bethan supposed she should be grateful too, but the whole scene had been nauseating, and she hated being taken for what she was not, even if the misunderstanding was of little consequence. But really, was she forever destined to be mistaken for a whore?

"Are you sure Angus and Murdo will be all right? I would hate for them to be hurt on my account."

"Aye. At two against twelve, they can pose no threat to anyone, and it was clear they were in no state to fight. The McDonalds have captured the prize they wanted, or so they think, so they won't bother about them. Instead, they will leave for the kirk as soon as...possible."

As soon as Malcolm had reached his pleasure, he meant.

Bethan swallowed hard. The day had not turned out quite how she expected it to.

"In a way, by giving them tainted food, it could be argued that Morag saved the two men's lives," she mused. Had the two warriors been able to stand their ground, their attackers might have thought it safer to kill them.

"It could. And she provided the perfect distraction. Thank the Lord for her greed and cunning." Cameron nudged his horse back into a canter. "Come. Let us try to reach Loch Rannoch before nightfall."

Chapter Thirteen

That night and the following nights, they slept in a clearing in the woods. To Cameron's delight, Bethan seemed to enjoy sleeping outdoors as much as he did and she never complained about the lack of comfort or the fact that she had no maid to assist her. This trip was even more enjoyable than the one up to Scotland had been because they were on their own and, unlike then, he didn't feel he was doing anything wrong. Reassured no one was after them, they were able to enjoy a leisurely pace.

The only thing that would have made the moment even better would have been spending their nights making love. But an odd shyness had seemed to settle between them. Bethan was no longer looking at him the way she had, with barely disguised longing. Cameron wasn't sure why that might be. Perhaps she wanted to be sure all her troubles were over before relaxing her guard, perhaps she could not forget how the night had ended the last time they had made love, when she had been attacked, and she needed time to get over the trauma.

Perhaps now that she had slaked the lust he stirred within her, she felt able to move on.

Or perhaps she regretted having surrendered to the desire she'd felt for him.

These last two explanations tore at his gut, but he forced himself to be reasonable. He couldn't think like that. It would only bring him pain as he was not sure what the reason for the change in her was anyway. Did *he* regret what had happened? Nay. Did *he* feel ready to move on to his next conquests? Nay. He couldn't wait for the next time Bethan allowed him to touch her. He would just have to wait until she was ready.

One morning they woke up surrounded by a thick fog. Up until then the weather had been glorious, and they had not had to worry about cold, rain or even wind, quite a feat considering the season. Today, it was most decidedly cold, and rain didn't seem far away. Bethan shivered and tightened her cloak around her. In the eerie, muffled atmosphere, everything seemed different. Even her mood seemed different, more subdued. She seemed lost in thought, almost dejected. He hated it and he kept wondering if he had done something wrong. But no matter how much he tried to, he couldn't think of anything.

"I realize I never thanked you for saving me that night in the bedchamber," he heard her say as he leaned to reach the saddle bag containing the loaf of bread they had bought the previous day. "Without you I would be McDonald's wife by now."

Bethan married to that bastard against her will? At his mercy night after night? The thought wrenched a growl out of Cameron. "You don't need to thank me. I was glad to be there."

For the tenth time he congratulated himself on having chosen that night to make her his. Resisting temptation for another day would not only have been foolish, but it could have had disastrous consequences. She would have been alone, at the mercy of McDonald and his men, for he had never thought she was in danger while within Crois Dhubh. He'd told her himself that a few lairds had started sniffing around, but how could he have guessed any would be so treacherous as to sneak in at night to abduct her? And how had they done it? Even though the place was not as well guarded as it should be, the men would have had to have inside help to manage the intrusion so discreetly. He hoped Angus and Murdo would have found out more by the time he got back.

Anger simmering, he chewed on his piece of bread.

"I should have guessed he would not be so easily defeated," Bethan said next, almost to herself.

Defeated? What was she talking about? How could she have guessed anyone would come find her in her room in the middle of the night? These were despicable methods only a scoundrel would have anticipated. If he had not thought about it, how could she have? Unless...

"Had you met the man before, then?"

Master McDuff had told him she'd received three visitors the day before the attack, he now remembered. Had McDonald been one of them? Had he threatened to come to her in the night? And if so, why had she not mentioned it?

"I...'Tis nothing."

The hairs at the back of Cameron's neck started to prickle. His every instinct told him that it was most decidedly *not* nothing. For one, she had gone bright red, for another she looked as if she regretted having made the comment. She was hiding something, that much was obvious. Something he would hate to hear.

"What happened?"

"Nothing." His face must have made it clear she had better not ignore his question because she carried on, averting her gaze. "He had come to Crois Dhubh the day before along with two other lairds, and he pressed his suit on me, most forcefully."

Most forcefully. She meant he had pounced on her. An

image suddenly tore through his mind. The scratch on her neck he had seen the morning after the lairds' visit. She had not hurt herself trying to put on a veil, like she'd claimed, she been attacked by McDonald, damn the man's eyes!

"Did he—"

"No. Murdo stopped him, and there was no reason to think he would want to—"

This time Cameron shot to his feet. Had he heard that right? Murdo had known about the assault, and he'd not told him anything? What the hell was going on here? Didn't he think his laird had the right to know something like that? "I'll kill him for keeping such a thing secret from me!"

"You will no such thing!" Bethan protested, standing up in turn. "If you are going to take issue with anyone, it will have to be me. I asked him to keep silent; he did nothing wrong."

"Is that supposed to appease me?" he roared. "I am his laird, he should have told me, regardless of what you made him swear. If I'd known what had happened, that bastard McDonald would not have been able to sneak inside the castle that night, this much I can tell you. Had I been warned, I would have put a man outside your door to keep guard, I would have told everyone to— Fuck, Bethan! I would not have had you assaulted a second time for the world!"

He tore at his hair. Couldn't she see how much of a blow this was for him? She was under his care, how was he supposed to ensure her safety if he wasn't told what the situation was?

"I was not assaulted a second time," Bethan said soothingly. Maybe she had seen how affected he was, and no wonder. He was fuming. "He only grabbed my ankle that night. And like the first time, he was stopped before anything could happen. You protected me. There's no harm done."

No harm done... That was where they disagreed. Pity the

bastard was now dead. Cameron would have liked nothing better than to kill him a second time for what he'd done.

Bethan placed a tentative hand on his arm. He took a step back. He could not bear her touch, not now. He wasn't sure whether he wanted to shake her for keeping such a secret from him or tumble her to the ground to kiss her senseless. Neither would be wise.

"Any more secrets you're keeping from me?" he asked bitterly. He'd thought after an unpromising start, that they had come to trust one another. Why had she wanted to keep such a thing from him? "Like why you do not seem to want to touch me anymore?"

She reddened. "I... To tell you the truth I thought *you* didn't want *me*. You haven't tried to kiss me or anything for days."

No, he had not, because he was no fool and neither was he a lecher like McDonald, who was not above ignoring a woman's wishes to get his way. He could sense she would resist this time if he drew her into his arms, so he had kept his hands to himself. But after the revelation she had just made, he was wondering if she was not hiding something else from him. Something terrible. And he didn't like it one little bit.

He stuffed the bread back in the bag, his appetite having quite deserted him.

"Let's ride."

The day was spent in a somewhat tense atmosphere, and Cameron knew it was not due to the mist which continued to follow them.

"You still haven't told me what you were doing that night at the tavern," he told her that evening, once they had sat down next to a roaring fire.

Bethan had evaded the question once and he had allowed her to, but he needed an answer now. After all they had gone through together, and their night of passion, they were no longer strangers. And after this morning's revelation he needed to see she trusted him with her secrets.

Besides, there was no reason for her to be shy. He suspected her visit had something to do with a man, and since he now knew about her lovers, there was no need to keep silent.

After a brief hesitation she answered.

"I had gone to see Mistress Elen. Working with…well, with women who sell their bodies, she knows all there is to know about preventing conception."

He nodded. He'd already guessed she would take precautions, as the last thing she would have wanted was going to the altar with a swollen stomach. It was one thing pretending to still be untouched, quite another to explain away a child.

A child…

Cameron stiffened when a thought struck him. Had she used the woman's skill to rid herself of an unwanted baby? It was very possible. A woman taking lovers as she did could all too easily have fallen with child, perhaps even more than once.

"Did Mistress Elen ever help you get rid of an unborn babe?"

"No!" Bethan looked so horrified that he instantly knew she was telling the truth. He took in a deep breath, reassured. "I swear I never conceived, thanks to the draughts she gave me every full moon. That evening, I had gone to tell her I was leaving for Scotland."

And wouldn't require her services anymore.

His heart leaped to his throat as another, shocking thought exploded in his mind.

The solar, her bedchamber… He had not taken any precautions while bedding her because he'd been convinced that a woman of her experience would know how to guard herself against unwanted consequences. And he'd been right, she had. Except that, unlike her other lovers, he had bedded her at a time when she had imagined she would be married—in other words, when she did not need to worry about falling with child.

Honesty compelled him to add that he would probably not have tried to withdraw even if he'd not thought it safe. Their lovemaking had been too passionate, too intense, he'd been too lost to his desire to think about anything other than his need for her. But it could now have devastating consequences.

The fool! Had he given her more than just pleasure that day?

"Did you stop taking the draughts when we set off for Crois Dhubh?" he asked slowly.

Bethan froze as Cameron's meaning hit her. She'd stopped taking the draughts the day she'd received the letter informing her of the arrival of the Scots. It was one thing preventing her lovers' seed from taking root, but she did not want to prevent her lawfully wedded husband from making her with child. Like most women, she wanted children. Only, she wanted legitimate children who would not suffer from her folly so she'd made sure to follow her friend's instructions to the letter. But knowing she wouldn't need it any longer, she'd left her pouch of herbs behind when they'd set off for Crois Dhubh.

Which meant she had been unprotected when she had welcomed Cameron inside her body.

She looked at him, trying not to let her dismay show. Up until then it had never even crossed her mind that their fiery encounters could bear fruit. Used to knowing she had the protection of the herbs, she had never stopped her lovers from reaching their pleasure inside her body. Undeniably, this time she had been foolishly complacent. But her lovemaking with Cameron had been so overwhelming, it had felt so inevitable, she had not stopped to think it could end up in a disaster.

With her other lovers, she had not let herself be carried away thus. It had been completely different. She had selected them, lured them in, chosen the right moment to join them in bed, and she'd prepared herself in advance in accordance with Mistress Elen's advice. With Cameron, things had escaped her control. Their lovemaking had been raw, animalistic, a claiming, nothing like the careful seduction she was used to. There had been nothing premeditated about it, it had been a call of the senses. The first time he had taken her up against a wall, for goodness' sake! Reason, restraint, caution, everything had been burned away by need. All that had counted had been desire. Even afterward, in her bed, it had been all about passion and pleasure. And she hadn't thought about the consequences.

Dear God.

Considering how virile Cameron was and how many times he'd taken her, it would be a miracle if she was not with child. Dare she hope the effect of the herbs had still not vanished from her body? Of course not. Almost two months had passed since she had received the letter. Mistress Elen had been very clear. They only worked if you took them regularly, and even then, accidents could happen.

So what if she was with child? What would she do?

"You'll have to marry me if you are carrying my child," Cameron said slowly. It was as if he'd heard her question and didn't want her to wonder what would happen for longer than necessary.

"I... Marry you?"

"Aye, don't think I will not face my responsibilities."

"I'm thinking nothing of the sort." Still, it was a bit hasty, was it not?

And then it hit her like a bolt of lightning. What appeared hasty to her wouldn't to someone who'd premeditated the whole thing.

"Bethan? What is it?" Cameron asked, worry etched on his face. "Are you all right?"

No, she was not all right, and she could well imagine all color had drained from her face. But his concern only brought bile to her throat. He dared act solicitously when he was just like the others.

How had she not seen he was not really interested in *her*, only in her money? The clues had been there, even if she had missed them. He had come to her barely two days after his nephew's funeral, when it had been established she was no longer a poor woman. He had repeatedly taken her that day, first in the room at the back of the solar and then in bed, and yet he had never once seemed worried about the consequences or apologized for his lack of control. He had insisted on going with her all the way to Wales so as to keep an eye on her and see if she missed her courses when surely, as laird, his presence was required in Scotland. He had not tried to touch her since they'd left, hoping he had already done what was needed to get her with child and wouldn't have to renew an experience that had only been a means to an end.

How could she have been so stupid?

"You never wanted me," she said in a deathly voice. "You're only after my new fortune."

Cameron looked as if she had slapped him. "What? No! I swear." When she made to turn away, he grabbed her by the shoulders to force her to look at him. His eyes had gone dark with intent. "How can you even think this? I did want you, more than I have ever wanted anyone in my life, I still want you. How can you doubt it, after what happened in the solar? In your bed afterward? Of have you forgotten all that?"

Forgotten? How could she have forgotten the best moments of her life? But now she was finding out that she had been the only one swept away in the moment, whereas all the while he'd had an ulterior motive.

"Oh, no I haven't forgotten!" she cried out, pushing him

away so she could scramble back to her feet. She could not stay so close to him, she could not let his proximity blunt her fury or blur her understanding. "But all that happened *after* you had found out Dougal had written his will in my favor. Once I was a rich woman. Just like Donald and Malcolm McDonald, you hoped to—"

"No!" Cameron repeated, before shooting back to his feet in turn. "I'm nothing like those bastards, do you hear! Look me in the eye and tell me I forced you into anything, if you dare."

She could not do that because he had not forced her in any way. But how could she believe he had not used the desire she felt for him to his advantage? He had been awfully quick to offer a solution to her predicament, had he not, a predicament they weren't even sure she was in. No sooner had she mentioned the draughts—or lack thereof—than he had told her she would have to marry him. A normal man would have panicked at the idea that their single night of passion might have borne fruit, asked her if she could be mistaken, done anything to convince her—and themselves—that it might not come to that.

Cameron had simply said she would have to marry him. It was hard not to think it was what he'd been hoping for all along.

There was only one thing to do. She had to lie, leave him under no illusion that he would get his way.

"I'm sorry to disappoint you but there is no chance that I am carrying your bastard." They both winced at the word, but she carried on. "I never stopped taking the draughts, because I wanted time to get to know Dougal before I gave birth to his child. I had planned to stop only when I felt comfortable in my new life." Would he believe her? It was not impossible. He did not know about her desire for children, and it would make sense that she would wait until she had found her place at Crois Dhubh to become a mother. "So you see, there will be no need to marry me. I'm afraid you will have to find yourself another rich wife."

"I don't want a wife, rich or otherwise!" he roared. "If I did, I would be married by now, don't you think? I'm one and thirty, for heavens' sake, not twenty! Bethan. Listen to me. I did not rape you, or abduct you, or bed you just to get you with child, and I care not about your money. I am nothing like the men who are after you." He had never sounded so irate, so bitter at the same time. "I went to you because I could not resist you a moment longer, nothing more. But if you are with child, then of course we will have to marry. It's the only honorable thing to do."

"Listen to *you*, Cameron!" Bethan was angry and bitter herself. "How am I supposed to believe you want me? You tell me you do not want a wife, and then in the same breath you tell me we'll have to marry all the same. This is not what a woman wants to hear." Not what she wanted to hear, anyway.

"How about the connection between us? Do not deny that it exists. It was there from the moment we met. That night at the tavern, you wanted me as much as I wanted you."

"Yes. I did," she acknowledged brazenly. She would not let him place the blame on her or make her feel ashamed. "And you knew it. Yet you did not touch me, did not kiss me. Until I became a rich woman, you had no difficulty keeping your urges under control. You did not act on your desire for me."

"Christ, of course, I did not act on it! What kind of a man do you take me for? It wouldn't have been right. I was escorting you to your future husband, my own nephew! In those circum-stances, I could hardly allow myself to be overwhelmed by my desire for you."

"Why not? You knew I was no longer an innocent virgin," she argued. "I was already ruined for my husband. Another man in my bed would have made little difference."

"God's blood! *Another* man! Stop making yourself sound like the most seasoned harlot!" Cameron erupted. "Of course, our lovemaking would have been different. None of your other lovers had been your betrothed's uncle, as far as I know?"

This was an irrefutable argument, but Bethan was so raw, she felt so betrayed that she refused to be pacified so easily. They remained on either side of the fire, glaring at each other, the heat of the flames the perfect illustration of the anger boiling inside them.

"You said the other day that I was now free to choose my husband and I will," she said defiantly "This time I will not let any man dictate my future, for whatever reason, however much they want to sway me with their skill in bed."

"I did not try to—"

"You have escorted me out of Scotland, ensuring that I did not fall into the arms of Malcolm McDonald or anyone else," she cut in. "I thank you for that, but I am now safe from them. So tomorrow I will take my leave and carry on alone."

Wales was still some distance away, but she was not far from Sheridan Manor, a two days' ride at the most. There she would find men to ride with her to Castell Esgyrn. Or she could go to William... After having been made a knight, he had been given a modest castle on the other side of the forest. Yes. That was even better. Her friend would welcome her with no questions asked and keep her presence in England a secret.

"You will do no such thing," Cameron snapped.

"All danger of abduction has passed. I can very well—"

"This is not a request, Ealasaid. You might be free from unscrupulous Scottish lairds now that we're in England, but you'd still be a woman traveling on her own if I left you. 'Tis not safe."

Bethan's shoulders sagged. There would be no arguing with Cameron in this mood. She'd always been wise enough to choose her battles and knew she would never win this one. Besides, he was right. It was dangerous for a woman, rich or not, to be alone and unprotected on the road. She would be foolish to insist and put pride above security.

"Very well."

Without a word, she sat back down on the ground and settled herself for the night, doing her best to keep her tears at bay. How could it end this way? But what else had she hoped for? Parting ways with Cameron now or in a week's time, once they had reached Wales, would change little. They were destined to go their separate ways in the end. And if she had briefly entertained the notion that there could be a future for them, then it only showed that she really was a fool.

She would wait until she was closer to William's castle to slip away. Having never heard of her friend, Cameron wouldn't know where to look for her. Even if he went to Sheridan Manor because he remembered it was the English seat of the Hunter family, he would only be told that no one had seen her. It would be as if she had vanished into thin air. Yes, it was the perfect solution.

Now all she had to do was to convince her heart that she was happy with that decision.

~

The wretched woman!

Throwing another log into the fire, Cameron cursed Bethan for the thousandth time. How could she inflict such worry on him? He hadn't slept properly for three nights, ever since he had woken up one morning and found the nest where she had curled up the evening before empty.

The two days before her disappearance had been tense, which was little wonder considering their heated arguments the day of the mist, but he had forced himself to patience. Bethan was no fool, but an uncommonly sensible and honest woman. Confident she would eventually calm down and understand that he had not tried to trap her into anything, he had wanted to give her the time she needed to deal with the events of the past few weeks in her own time. It had been an upheaval, undoubtedly, but she would see that he was nothing like those bastards who'd thought to rape and abduct her. He had taken her to bed because he had been unable to resist the torturing desire he felt for her, desire she shared, no matter how much she pretended she didn't.

But less than three days later, she had vanished into thin air.

Where the devil had she gone? He had scoured the countryside around, to no avail, and was doing his best to convince himself she had found a hiding place, rather than been attacked and left for dead in a ditch. Why, oh, why, had he not tied her to a tree before going to sleep each night? It would have been safer.

Cameron let out a snort. Of course, he could not have done such a thing as tie a woman to a tree! He was losing his mind. But he desperately wanted to find her, know that she was all right.

After a week of ceaseless wanderings, he understood that he would never find her. His chest churning with anger, resentment, and frustration, he gave up the search and went back home. If she wanted to punish him for doing nothing more than trying to take his responsibility, then let her. He was done acting like an idiot and would not be manipulated a moment longer.

But as the leaves on the hills around Nead an Diabhail turned from vivid green to burnt orange, Cameron understood that he would never be able to let it go. He could not live his life not knowing what had happened to his Ealasaid. Then one day a conversation with Murdo reminded him that there was somewhere she could have taken refuge.

Sheridan Manor, Connor Hunter's English seat. Of course... How had he not guessed that was where she would have gone? It had been less than a half day's ride away from the place he'd last seen her. It could not be a coincidence. Hope surged through him, bringing life flowing back in his veins.

The following morning, he was back on his horse, galloping on the road to England.

Chapter Fourteen

"I'm sorry, but we haven't seen Bethan in almost a year."

Cameron stared at Matthew Hunter, Lord Sheridan's brother, refusing to accept what he was being told, that he had come all the way here for nothing. It couldn't be. "Do you ken if she has gone back to Castell Esgyrn?" he asked, trying his best not to let his dismay show.

It would make sense if she had. If he had to push on all the way to Wales to see her, then he would do it. He would not go back home before he had explored all possible options and found out her whereabouts because he knew he would never be able to settle otherwise.

"I'm sorry, but I don't think she has. I received a letter from Connor two days ago. He would have mentioned it if she had appeared out of nowhere. In fact, I'm surprised to hear you asking about her. We all thought she was in Scotland with her husband."

"Aye. Of course."

There it was. His last hope, had gone up in smoke. No one from her family seemed to have heard of her. What did it mean? Was she safe, and hiding somewhere he couldn't think of? Had she gone to her brother? Or was she dead, as he'd feared many times?

Lord, please let her not be dead.

He fell on the bench behind him, all efforts at hiding his emotions gone. If Bethan was really dead, then he didn't know how he would bear it. He had missed her terribly these last three months. Missed her and ranted against her. Damn her for being cruel enough to disappear without a trace and causing him endless worry, for being too stubborn to see that he had done nothing wrong by offering to marry her if she was with child. What else should he have done? Leave her to deal with his lack of control alone? Force her to bear the shame of giving birth to a bastard child?

Of course, he had offered to do the honorable thing, how could he not? But she had assumed the worst of him, misunderstanding his motives. Instead of acknowledging that their love-making had been inevitable, given the heat that had sparked between them from the moment they had met, she had accused him of bedding her to trap her into a union she didn't want, of being no better than those McDonald whoresons. How could she think that, never mind say it out loud? Hadn't she felt the connection between them? Hadn't she given herself to him wholeheartedly?

The wretched woman. He had no idea what he would do when—if—he saw her again. Smother her with kisses or give her the tongue lashing of her life.

Matthew Hunter seemed to take pity on him. "We could go ask my former squire, Sir William Parry. He knows Bethan, who's been a frequent visitor over the years. It's not impossible that he might have heard of her."

Cameron shot up to his feet, hope fanned anew. If one of her friends lived nearby, it was not inconceivable she would have gone to him to ask for help. Maybe this William would know where she was. Now that Matthew had mentioned him, he remembered hearing the name in Bethan's mouth. What had she said about the man? He could not recall, but it made little difference. All that mattered was going to see if he could help them.

"Is it far? Can we go now?"

Matthew exchanged a glance with his wife, a dark-haired woman with extraordinary amber eyes. She nodded slightly, as if she'd understood something no one had said. "It's not that far," was the answer she gave him.

"And yes, we can go now."

They found the castle brimming with activity. In the lists, a dozen men were sparring in full armor, squires and pages were cheering on the side, grooms were watching and taking bets on the outcome of the fights.

Matthew and Cameron waited, admiring the warriors who displayed well-honed skills. Which one was Bethan's friend?

After a while, a knight appeared in front of them, panting hard, his helm tucked under his arm. Tall and broad, with golden hair and chiseled features, he was every woman's fantasy come true. Jealousy, this ugly creature, reared its head. If this was Sir William Parry, the man Bethan had fled to, it seemed unavoidable that she would have shared his bed.

Oblivious to his musings, Matthew Hunter gave the younger man a paternal tap on the shoulder. "William, apologies for disturbing you in the middle of training." So this was indeed Sir William. Jealousy bared its fangs. It would not be long before it started to rip at his throat. "Let me introduce you to Laird Cameron Campbell, come from Scotland. He has a question to ask you."

The blond man arched a brow, as if the name surprised him. "Laird Campbell? Are you Dougal Campbell's uncle perchance?"

Hope fluttered inside Cameron's chest, wiping all other considerations from his mind. The man was indeed familiar with Bethan's life if he knew about her connection with his family. It was all that mattered. "Aye."

"I will say that you are not quite how I imagined you to be."

It was when Sir William eyed him up with obvious appreciation that Cameron remembered what Bethan had told him about her friend. He was the one who had refused to be her first lover because he liked men, not women. Well, if that was the case, he could rest easy. The two of them had not slept together, not now, or ever. Jealousy went back to its lair, its tail tucked between its legs.

"Nay, I imagine I'm not." Likely the word uncle would have conjured up images of grizzled old men in the man's mind.

"Would this question of yours wait a moment?" The knight gestured at his breastplate. "I'll admit I'll feel better once I've had a wash."

No, it can't wait. And you don't need to be clean to tell me if you know where Bethan is.

"Of course," Cameron said, nevertheless.

It did not take him long to regret his gracious answer. That night a banquet was given in honor of the knights who had competed in the afternoon, and midway through the meal, he still hadn't had the chance to talk privately with their host. As soon as Sir William had appeared, dressed in impeccably clean clothes, his hair falling in graceful curls over his shoulders, he'd been set upon by his guests. Everyone, it seemed, had something to tell him or congratulations to offer. A little delay Cameron could have handled, but this was sorely testing his patience.

"Well done on a victory well-earned this afternoon, my friend." A man raised his cup of mead in Sir William's direction.

"I thank you, but there is little merit in beating men twice my age and half my strength, don't you think?"

Laughter erupted in the hall. "Careful, pup!" the man holding the mead warned, his lips twitching. "I am not so old and weak that I cannot make you regret your impudence."

"I know it. But if you're really intent on offering your congratulations, then you might as well know that I am to be married soon. I believe it is a much more worthy reason for celebration." He paused for effect, a smile playing on his lips. "Before the month is over I shall be fortunate enough to call a beautiful lady my wife."

The raised eyebrows around the room told Cameron that the men, like him, were aware of Sir William's preferences, preferences that made this announcement somewhat of a shock.

"Congratulations," a man with his face mottled by drink grumbled. "Though if you really do have to marry for appearances' sake, you might at least have left this beautiful lady to someone who would actually enjoy having her in his bed."

"Hear, hear."

The murmur was not hostile, merely mocking. Clearly the men assembled tonight were friends that could be trusted not to hold his preferences against him.

Sir William smiled. "I will admit that I am perhaps not the best judge in such matters, but I have no choice but to say that the future Lady Parry is a ravishing beauty. It is not her only accomplishment, however. She is also learned, generous and quick-witted."

A tall man laughed. "I see! You intend to spend your evenings *talking* to your wife!"

"I most certainly do," he agreed tranquilly, ignoring the taunt. "For conversations with Bethan ferch Morgan are most enlivening."

With those words, he stared straight at Cameron, a clear provocation.

It took every ounce of control for him to remain in his seat, and his fingers tightened painfully around his tankard of ale. Had it been made of glass, it might well have shattered. Two emotions warred within him. The first one was relief. Bethan was clearly alive and well. She had made it, she had not been attacked, raped, and killed, as he'd feared many times. The second, much more powerful emotion assailing his gut was fury. She was to marry Sir William? What the hell was going on? The man didn't love her, he did not even want her, not in that way, at least, and she knew it. Why on earth had she agreed to this parody of a union? If this was her way of placing herself out of unscrupulous men's reach, then why marry only now, months after her disappearance, when the most pressing danger was gone?

He skewered Sir William with a dark stare, making it clear their talk would not be postponed any longer. Now he understood why the man had recognized his name... Bethan would have mentioned him. Heaven only knew what she had told her friend—her future husband, he should say. Well, he would make sure to add his own version to the story without further ado.

Very deliberately, he stood up and nodded toward the door, his meaning clear.

Come meet me, now.

"Careful, my laird. William is a good man, and I've known him since he was a child," he heard Matthew Hunter say under his breath. "Whereas I don't know you. If you harm him in any way, I will hunt you down and make you regret me giving you a chance."

The threat was not an idle one. Despite being his senior by two decades, the man was clearly still a formidable warrior.

"Fear not. I just have a few questions to ask him."

With those words, he made his way to the door. When Sir William walked out of the hall a moment later, Cameron was waiting for him in the middle of the bailey. Silently, he ordered him toward the stable. This conversation needed no witnesses. As soon as they were both inside, he leaned into the door frame, blocking any possible retreat. He knew that it did not take much effort for him to appear menacing, and he was glad of it.

"Now that you've had your wash, we'll have that talk, you and I."

Sir William did not appear in the least worried by his imposing stature and disgruntled voice.

"I suppose we will, since you're asking so nicely." His voice was calm when many lesser men would have flinched. Cameron's respect for him increased begrudgingly. "You know, I will have to trust what my wife says once we are married. She did mention that you could be gruff at times but, silly me, I put it down to the unusual situation you were in. Were I in your position, I, too, would have been on edge. She also said that you were remarkably handsome, but as she and I do not have quite the same idea of beauty, I'll admit that I did not set much score by her assessment. Now, however, I can see that Beth was right on both accounts."

Beth.

The nickname thrown in so naturally told Cameron that Sir William had not lied when he had claimed to be betrothed to Bethan. People gave each other special names to show their affection. Hadn't he himself taken to calling her Ealasaid because he'd felt a special connection to her? Hope died in his chest. For a moment, he had wondered if the man had not announced his betrothal to provoke his guests. He now could see that it had been no jest. Those two were indeed about to get married.

Which meant he had to act, fast.

"Where is she?" he growled. That was all he wanted to know.

"Where do you think? Here, of course. As you heard, we are about to be married."

Cameron recoiled. All this while, Bethan had been here, hidden away in one of the castle rooms? He'd been waiting patiently all night for a word with Sir William, hoping to find out where she had gone, and now he was being told he could have seen her hours ago? It was not to be borne.

He took a step forward. "Take me to—"

"Not now, she's asleep. I haven't told her you were here. She needs rest and she would never have gotten it after a conversation with you." Despite the flippant tone, it was clear there would be no convincing the man. Sir William was a formidable adversary, for all his tranquil ways. "I can take you to her tomorrow. She will be thrilled to see you... I think."

This was getting weirder by the moment. "You think your betrothed will be thrilled to see me, and you know why, yet you are willing to let me see her?"

A shrug answered him. "Of course. She's not my captive. If you have come, as I hope, to claim her, and she is brave enough to have you, then I will have nothing to say."

Cameron was not often rendered speechless, but he was now. The man was hoping his future wife would forsake him in favor of another man?

"Didn't you just say you were set to marry her?" he asked when he had finally regained his ability to talk. Surely he had not misunderstood.

"I did. We will, as I announced in the hall, be wed before the month is out."

In other words, in less than a week. "Why? You do not love her, she does not love you."

"Come, Laird Campbell." Sir William was not in the least daunted by his aggressive tone. He sounded amused, perhaps even faintly condescending. "It would hardly be the first time a bride and groom went to the altar without feeling love for each other. Besides, I might not love Beth in that way, but I do care for her and will not allow anyone to hurt her, even brawny Scots who think they can use her for their benefit."

This time there was a steely edge under the pleasant voice. The man was not quite as detached as he wanted to appear, and Cameron could well believe he would prove a mighty opponent. He'd seen him fight that very afternoon and win each of his combats. It seemed he was just as ruthless in life. But Cameron could be ruthless and formidable too, especially when so much was at stake. He was not going to stand here and be insulted when he had done nothing wrong. Whatever Bethan had told her friend, he had never intended to use her. He'd tried to tell her as much, but she'd refused to listen.

Well, she would listen now, he would make sure of it.

"I have no intention of hurting her," he said through gritted teeth.

"You might not have any *intention* of doing so but it doesn't follow that you will not."

Cameron bit the stringent retort already on his lips, since his meeting with Bethan depended on this infuriating man. Antagonizing him now wouldn't serve his purpose. Damn it all! If Sir William didn't want him to see Bethan, then he would not be able to get to her. She might not be a captive, but at the moment she didn't know he was here—and he had no idea in which room to find her.

What the hell was going on here, he asked himself for the tenth time? She was aware her friend preferred men, and yet she was ready to become his wife, therefore condemning herself to a life of frustration. Unless she intended to carry on as she had while betrothed to Dougal once she was married... She had claimed her intention to be faithful to his nephew, but this was different. Her English husband might well agree that her taking lovers was the best solution for both of them, in the circumstances.

Well, over his dead body.

If she was to take a man to her bed, it would be none other than himself, who would give her what she needed. And if she was that desperate to marry to escape men's greed, then he would...

Cameron stilled. What was he thinking? Was he really about to propose to Bethan a second time? He had not set out from Scotland with the intention of bringing her back home as Lady Campbell, but it now seemed the only thing to do, the only way to prevent her from making a dreadful mistake—and the only way to put an end to his suffering.

He'd once dreaded having to witness her wedding to his insipid nephew, he'd then had to see her being assaulted by one McDonald brother before narrowly escaping abduction by the other. After that, he could not bear to let her slip through his fingers once more.

Or ever.

Sir William cared for her? Well, he did too, more than cared.

He had told her three months ago that he didn't want a wife but would marry her if she was with child. She had taken it badly, perhaps with reason, and refused. He would tell her now that he did want a wife, and would marry her because he could not live without her and he would make damn well sure she accepted. Surely, when she saw he was offering for her hand when she was not with child and nothing obliged him to, she would understand he'd never meant to trap her into anything.

"Very well. Let her get the rest she needs," he said in a growl. "I will sleep here in the stables, out of the way. But then tomorrow morning I will see her, make no mistake about it."

And I will convince her to have me, instead of you.

Though he could not have missed the real meaning behind his words, Sir William nodded.

True to his word, shortly after dawn, Sir William came to inform him Bethan was up, and about to break her fast in the hall.

"You can join her. I will leave you two alone."

"No. Let her eat first," Cameron surprised himself by saying. Remembering how hungry she always was in the mornings, he wanted to make sure she had enough to eat before they met. Because once she had seen him, her appetite would be gone, he was certain of it. "Come and get me when she's ready."

He would have a quick wash in the meantime. For this, the most important discussion of his life, he needed to look and feel at his best.

It was not long before he was led to the hall, which was empty save for a woman sitting on a folding chair by the fire. Her back was to the door, and she was strangely immobile. It was obvious she wasn't eating, sewing, petting a dog, or doing anything other than staring at the flickering flames. It unnerved Cameron. Bethan had always been full of life, bursting with energy. Seeing her so still was unnatural.

Sir William gestured to him to wait and approached her alone. "Beth." He placed a gentle hand on her shoulder. "There's someone here to see you."

"I don't want to see anyone," Bethan answered, not moving an inch. Cameron barely recognized her voice, and no wonder. She had never sounded so lifeless. His unease grew. Was something ailing her? Was that why she needed rest? Was she ill?

"I know, sweetheart. But I think you need to see this man,

which is why I haven't thrown him out of here just yet. He's come a long way."

"Has he?" There was more than a hint of trepidation in those two words, as if she didn't dare hope. Cameron's heart started to beat faster. At last, a glimpse of the woman he'd come to know and love.

"Yes. He's waiting to take you on a stroll in the lists. Here, take this. 'Tis cold outside."

Sir William wrapped the cloak he was holding around her shoulders before placing the hood above her head. The gesture was protective, tender. It was obvious he hadn't been lying when he'd said he cared for her. Cameron couldn't help a surge of resentment from coursing through him. Bethan was allowing this man to take care of her, when she had all but fled from him for doing nothing more than what was right. She had taken refuge in her friend's home and asked him to marry her instead of turning to him for the protection she needed.

She would have a lot of explaining to do.

Bethan stood up at last and turned around—only to sag against Sir William when she saw who was standing in the door frame. Cameron almost ran to her, but the Englishman brought his arm around her in support before he could move.

"It's all right, he's not going to hurt you," her friend murmured in her ear.

What the devil? Of course, he would not hurt her! Why would they think that? And since when did he need permission to approach her? Dear God, when had things become so diffi-cult between them? Didn't she remember all they had shared?

"I'm not going to hurt you. But I need to talk to you," he said, taking a step forward. He would not be made to feel like a monster when he had done nothing wrong. "Please."

For a moment it looked as if she would agree. Then her eyes

filled with tears, and he knew all hope was lost. She shook her head.

"I'm sorry, I-I can't."

With those words, she turned and fled, leaving Cameron rooted to the spot.

The sound of footsteps behind him caused Cameron's heart to flip in his chest. Finally! After the disastrous encounter with Bethan this morning, Sir William had promised he would talk to her, convince her to give him a chance to explain himself. And it would seem he had succeeded. Gratitude flooded through him. They couldn't have left things the way they had. He needed to understand, he needed to explain himself, he needed...her.

Seeing her this morning, though it had been brief, though her face had been half hidden under the hood of her cloak, though she had appeared shocked to see him, had made him realize that he would not be able to breathe until he had made her see they belonged together.

"Ealasaid?" The word died on his lips when he turned around and saw Sir William standing in the middle of the room instead of the woman he wanted to see.

"I'm sorry, I don't know any Gaelic," the Englishman said. "What did you say?"

Cameron waved the question away. It was better the man had not understood the word had been nothing more than his pet name for Bethan. This was humiliating enough as it was. Because, evidently, she had not agreed to a meeting with him. Why? Surely she was not really afraid of him?

"I can't believe she's refusing to see me," he said through gritted teeth. How odd it was to confide in the man who was about to make the woman he wanted his wife. But what other choice did he have? Matthew Hunter had gone back to Sheridan Manor after the banquet, and anyway, Cameron hardly knew the man. Sir William was the only one who might understand how he felt, since he seemed to know the history between them. "Something has changed. She is not the woman I remember."

"Ah. Mayhap she is not."

What the hell did that mean? Cameron had had enough of this. He planted himself in front of the man who would marry Bethan in less than a week if he didn't put a stop to the madness. It was time to be blunt. He had once balked at the idea of her marrying Dougal because she needed a real man in her bed. Well, this would be ten times worse. Bethan was about to shackle herself to a man who could never satisfy her womanly needs. An inexperienced boy might have learned to please her in time, but a man who felt no desire for the female form would never be able or willing to give her what she craved.

"Listen. I know you and Bethan will never consummate your union, and I know why. So why the devil would you want to marry her, if not for her money? And why did she agree to such an unsatisfactory bargain? Something is not right here. If I didn't know better, I would say that she feels obliged to marry you. But you do not seem like a tyrant, and you obviously care about her. No," he said almost to himself. "She is not here under duress, at least that much is clear."

"Of course she's not. I would never do anything to harm her. We have known each other all our lives, or very nearly."

"That doesn't answer my question. Why would she want to marry a man who will never be a husband to her when she refused to marry me?" he said, running a hand through his hair in exasperation. "She didn't seem to want protection then, and yet she has accepted yours, knowing you could never give her what she needed."

Whichever way you looked at it, it made no sense.

"There is only one thing she needs now, and it's not a lover in her bed, but marriage to a respectable man. Oh, my laird, how can you not see it? She had no choice but to accept my offer." Sir William said gently. He leaned in toward him, as if not to be overheard. "You were right, she *is* changed. She is with child. Your child, I would dare to venture, though she never confirmed my suspicions. Does that answer your question? She doesn't care about protecting herself, but she needs to protect her babe from malice, give it a name and a father."

Cameron stared at him in shock. Bethan was with child? He wouldn't be more stunned if he'd been hit over the head with one of Sir Alan's blasted maces.

"But she said she'd...she said she couldn't be..."

Had she lied then when she'd claimed to be still taking Mistress Elen's draughts? It was possible. He hadn't seen her drink anything while they were on the road, but perhaps she'd been too discreet, not wanting any of the men to guess what she was doing. That was very possible.

Hell, he couldn't think, and he desperately needed to. He needed to understand.

Sir William sighed, taking pity on him. "I suspect she lied because she was too hurt and wanted to protect her pride. She believes you're only after her fortune, and her feelings for you are too strong for her to accept that easily. My guess is that she wants far more from you. In any case, she is most definitely with child. Whether it's yours or not is—"

"The bairn is mine!" Cameron roared, unable to even hear the fact denied.

That babe was his, he knew it in his bones. Bethan would not have gone to another man mere days after the night of passion they had shared. Now he understood why she had been so hurt by his clumsy proposal. Sir William was right. Her feelings for him were strong, far stronger than she would have liked to admit, far stronger than his had been at the time, even. That was why she had surrendered to his desire so readily. And she would have been appalled to see that he was only offering to marry her out of duty when she would have accepted him out of love.

What a mess. His insides felt as if they had been ripped apart by a wild cat.

His agony must have shown on his face because Sir William sighed again, like a man torn between showing loyalty to a friend and doing what his conscience was urging him to do.

"She's in the herb garden just outside the postern gate. Go to her and beg her not to gut me for revealing what she was desperate to keep from you. Then offer for her again, making it clear why you're doing it this time. If she will have you instead of me, I won't stand in your way. As you know, my feelings are not engaged in this affair, only my deepest affection and a desire to save her reputation and give her child a name. I will easily relinquish the honor of looking after her to the man who will be a far better husband that I could ever be."

Cameron placed his hand on Sir William's shoulder, knowing that from now on he would count the man amongst his dearest friends. He'd been prepared to offer Bethan—and his unborn child—the protection they needed. It was clear that he had done so solely for her sake, not to put an end to malicious rumours concerning the way he'd chosen to live his life. If he'd wanted to do that, he would be long married by now.

"For everything you did, you have my eternal gratitude."

Sir William rolled his eyes to the sky and gave a mock sigh. "Your gratitude. Yes. I guess that is all I will ever get from you, so I will have to be content with it. Now, go."

Chapter Fifteen

There she was, sitting on a wooden bench, alone, staring into the distance, her profile pure and delicate against the backdrop of burned leaves and swirling skies.

Cameron drank her in. How he had missed her, how precious she was to him, doubly so now that he'd been told about the bairn she was about to give him. She had changed clothes since that morning and was now wearing a simple woolen gown and a tight wimple. An odd choice for a young, unmarried woman, one who never wore veils. It framed her face completely, covering even her forehead and cheeks. In the severe headdress she looked like a widow.

Still achingly beautiful.

His gaze dropped to her stomach, but he could not detect any swelling under the heavy folds of her gown. It was early days yet, but perhaps she would feel different under his palm. As soon as she allowed him to draw her into his arms, he would splay his hands over her belly and meet his child. The thought was so dizzying he had to brace himself against the stone wall for fear he would collapse. A child with Bethan... Only a few days ago he'd not imagined she would ever be his wife and here he was, about to become a father—and a husband.

He cleared his throat, causing her to turn to face him. Panic flared in her eyes, followed by something else. Desire? Hope?

Not wanting her to balk again, he stayed where he was and waited for her to speak.

"Cameron."

He took a step forward. The cold tone was not exactly encouraging. But at least she had not called him "Laird Campbell." It was something.

"Ealasaid, you—"

"Don't call me that."

It was the first time she had prevented him from using his special name for her and it stung. But he understood why she would feel raw, so he kept silent.

She stood up, eyes flashing. "What are you doing here? How did you convince William to tell you where I was?" She shook her head, in anger or disappointment, he wasn't sure quite which. "I swear I will gut him for this."

There it was, the threat he'd been warned about.

Should he lie, protect the man from her ire, pretend he'd found her here on his own? No. There would be no misunderstanding between them from now on, no lies. Besides, he wanted her to know he had come with her friend's full agreement.

"I didn't need to convince him. He told me of his own accord where you were, since he, like me, is of the opinion that we should talk. He also told me to beg you not to gut him for doing so, a wise precaution, apparently, since you've already promised to do just that. So I'm begging you. Please don't gut him."

To his relief, her mouth quivered. Maybe all hope was not lost... If they could only talk, if he could only explain, if she could only trust him, if they could only recapture what had once been between them, then all would be well. There was no other choice, anyway. It was not just about the two of them now. They had their child to consider. The bairn needed them, *both* of them.

"Why did you flee that day, leaving me without a word of reassurance as to your whereabouts?" he asked, taking another step forward. "I worried myself sick, wondering what had happened to you, imagining the worst."

She had the good grace to appear guilty. "I know, I'm sorry but I had to leave. After what you did..."

"What was that? Ask you to marry me?" It was hard not to sound accusatory, but he still felt the sting of her rejection keenly. She had thought him as despicable as those rogues who wanted her fortune, not the woman she was, and it had hurt. True, he had not proclaimed his undying love when he'd offered to marry her, but there were worst slights to inflict on a woman than to tell her he would take responsibility for what he'd done.

"Yes."

Bethan could not forget—or forgive—that Cameron had come to her only once she had become a rich woman. As coincidences went, this one was hard to swallow. While they had ridden to Scotland, and she was of no consequence, he had not allowed his desire for her to overwhelm him, even though it had been obvious she shared it. Though she had to agree he felt something for the woman she was, rather than merely wanting the fortune she could bring him, it was hard not to conclude that he'd been swayed as much by her newfound fortune as by any affection he felt for her. And after the disaster of her betrothal to Dougal, she hadn't wanted to marry for any reason other than love. Alas, as could have been predicted, that luxury had been denied to her.

Because she had fallen with child from her encounters with the fiery Scot.

William had walked in on her one morning, emptying the contents of her stomach in the lists. When the same thing had happened three times in a row, there had been no hiding what was ailing her. Her friend had provided the support she had needed, uttering no judgment, offering to make her his wife without delay, even if people would guess that he could not be the father of this baby. He had made her see that he was her only hope at respectability and she'd been grateful for his offer. They weren't in love, admittedly, but at least they had the honesty to acknowledge it, and life with him would be more pleasant than with most men.

"You ken very well what motivated my offer of marriage," Cameron said, taking another step toward her. He was being very careful, as if he thought her a timid doe who could bolt at any time, not an unreasonable thought, she had to admit. She was fighting the urge to flee again and avoid the painful conversation.

"I do know what prompted your offer. And we both know it was not love."

He made a face she had difficulty interpreting. For a moment he looked on the verge of contradicting her, then he shook his head. "It was not greed either, unlike what you seemed to believe. I care not about your fortune."

"No."

At least she had the honesty to acknowledge this. He'd wanted to give the babe she might have conceived a name. It was an honorable intention, but she had the weakness of wanting more, of wanting to be chosen for herself, not because duty dictated he should marry her.

Honorable to the core and putting duty before pleasure. That was how he had described himself the day he had told her he'd not wanted to be laird, and his whole life had proved it. Well, she didn't want to be another burden he'd had to shoulder because there were no other options. It would only destroy whatever had started to bloom between them.

She could only congratulate herself on having had the presence of mind to pretend there was no chance she could fall with child that day, otherwise there would be no stopping him from marrying her now that she was indeed with child. Thank the Lord he had come to find her now, and not in three months' time, when it would have been impossible to hide her swollen stomach, or in the new year, when he might have found her with the babe at her breast.

Married or not, he would have bundled her up and whisked her away, straight back to Nead an Diabhail.

But why had he come at all? That was what she didn't understand. She had thought never to see him again. After finding her gone, she'd imagined he would go back to Scotland, and forget he'd ever met a Welshwoman who'd been supposed to marry his nephew. What did he hope to achieve by coming all the way here? How had he even known where she was? Did it matter? No. It was too late anyway. She had found a solution to her predicament, and she would not allow anyone to steer her away from the path she had chosen.

"In any case, soon I will not have to worry about any of that," she said, stiffening her spine. "I will be a married woman. I will be safe. Men will stop coveting my newfound fortune and lusting after me."

"Don't be so naïve. As Lady Parry, your fortune will indeed be out of reach but that will not stop men from pursuing you. Married or not, you will still draw them like a flame draws moths," Cameron said with more feeling that she had ever heard in his voice. "You are an extraordinarily beautiful woman, Ealasaid, and you know it. Having a husband might protect you from unwanted marriage proposals, but men will always lust after you. You told me they did when you were a virgin, and betrothed, they won't stop now that you cannot be ruined anymore, quite the opposite. Forgive me for saying as much, but you chose the worst husband to keep suitors at bay. Everyone will know you do not have a true marriage. Giving you what Sir William will never be able to give you will be too great a temptation to resist."

Bethan bit her bottom lip. He was right, unfortunately. She had attracted men's attention when she had been supposedly out of reach. Things would not change just because she had become Lady Parry. It was as Cameron had said. Her future husband's preferences were not quite as secret as she'd hoped, and men would know she did not get fulfillment in her marital bed. They would see it as a personal challenge to try and show her what she was missing. But she had a weapon at her disposal now, a weapon no one but William knew about.

"Men have lusted after me in the past, but they won't any longer, not with this." She tore at her wimple in a violent gesture, exposing her right cheek. "Look at me now and tell me I am an extraordinarily beautiful woman if you dare!"

A sob escaped her lips. William never made her feel self-conscious about the scar, but she knew she looked hideous. What would Cameron make of it? He would look at her differently, it was inevitable, and she could not deny that the notion tore at her gut. She had never thought that *he* would see what she had become. Tears welled in her eyes. Why, oh, why, did he have to come, disturb the fragile peace she was trying to find, reawaken the desire she felt for him—and make her feel like a monster?

Frozen in horror, Cameron stared at the long jagged scar on Bethan's cheek, a pink trail running from the corner of her right eye to her jaw, right under her earlobe. Now he understood why she had chosen to wear the strange wimple-like headdress. She had not wanted him to see the scar. He remembered how Sir William had placed the hood over her head earlier that day before she could turn around. He had not wanted him to see the scar either.

"Who shall I kill for this?" he growled, his hand going straight to the hilt of his sword.

He would not just kill the man, he would make him wish he'd never been born. The attack had to have happened in the last three months, because when he'd last seen her, her face had been unmarred.

"What happened? What bastard hurt you so? Just say the name."

"I... No one."

Cameron watched as Bethan cradled her cheek in her hand and his heart almost stopped. "You don't mean... You did that to yourself?"

She lowered her eyes to the ground, providing him with the answer.

She had.

"But why?" He was appalled. What could possibly have gone through her mind to make her do such a thing?

"The week after I arrived here, there was a storm. A peddler sought refuge at the castle for the night. He was a filthy old man, thin as a reed, and smelling worse than a pile of dung." She gave an involuntary shiver, as if the mere memory of that smell offended her nose. "He slept in the stables, keeping well out of the way. In the morning, before leaving, he tried to sell me various unguents and potions supposed to enhance a woman's beauty. I told him I didn't need anything. He laughed and told me beautiful women always said that, but then there came a time when they regretted not having done anything to preserve their youth and beauty while they could."

"What a bloody fool." Cameron was certainly not impressed by the man's attitude, but he did not see what that story had to do with anything. Surely Bethan had not slashed her face to prove to the old idiot that she would not mind losing her beauty —supposing she ever would?

"Seeing that there would be no convincing him, I lost patience and made to walk away. That was when he pounced."

Cameron's blood exploded in his veins, the strength of his fury making his eyeballs sting and his bones turn to ashes. Not again! Not another man thinking he could use her body for his pleasure! Where was the bastard now? If he wasn't dead already, he would find him and flay him alive, inch by excruciating inch, before stuffing his mouth full with his bloody unguents.

"Please tell me Sir William arrived in time to stop him?"

Before I start retching.

"There was no need. When he grabbed me, I was so overwhelmed with anger and disgust that I struck him down with his heavy wooden staff. I told you he was a wisp of a man, so it wasn't that hard." She raised her head, looking as fierce as a warrior queen. He had never been prouder of anyone than he was of her in this moment. "I believe I would have killed him had a groom not arrived at that moment."

"Aye, well, he deserved no less anyway."

"Perhaps. But I'm glad not to have a man's death on my conscience. I stopped him from—I stopped him, it is all that matters. But the attack shocked me. Donald McDonald, his brother, the peddler... Who would be next? And what would happen if the next man succeeded? I could not bear the idea of being raped or captured or forced to marry to a man I did not want, like I almost was three times in as many months." She put her fingertips on the scar. "So, I did what I could do to deter suitors."

"Dear God, Ealasaid."

Before he could think, Cameron drew her into his arms. Mercifully, she didn't stop him, because he needed to hold her, reassure himself she was unharmed. Would that he had been there for her, to make her see that she didn't have to resort to such extreme measures to be safe!

He brushed his forefinger along the raised ridge of the scar slicing her cheek in half. It did not look too deep a cut, as if she had not found the courage to do as much damage as she wished. Still, he could not imagine the pain she had endured. And the worse of it was, it had been for nothing. Because scar or no scar, she was still the most arresting woman he had ever seen. Her eyes had lost none of their sparkle. Her smile still had the power to steal his breath. And even if she had cut the other cheek, it would have made no difference. Her spirit was untouched, no matter what marks had appeared on her skin. Above all, it was what made her beautiful.

His chest tightened.

"You dared me to look at you and tell you you were an extraordinarily beautiful woman," he whispered, his mouth at her temple. "Well, I am looking at you and I cannot say otherwise. This is a scar, nothing more. It doesn't diminish your beauty in any way. You are still perfect to me. You're still the only woman I want."

He felt her sag against him, a sure sign her resolve was weakening. "Cameron, you must stop talking like that."

"Why? When it is nothing but the truth?"

"Because you weren't supposed to come back, you wretched man! You weren't supposed to care about me. But you did come back," she cried out. "And you... And now you're behaving as if you did care about me. It's too much. I don't know what to think anymore. I don't know what to do."

Hope swelled in his chest. She had seen how much he

cared, and it had broken through her defenses. "Don't think, *mo chridhe*, and just do what feels right. Stay with me, you know it's the right thing to do."

For a moment, Bethan looked as if she would answer—and instead, burst into tears. Without the least hesitation, he swept her into his arms and sat down on the bench behind them, keeping her cradled in his lap, closing his eyes when her familiar honeyed scent enveloped him. She wasn't usually prone to such outpourings of emotion. Was this a good sign? Dare he hope she was finally surrendering to her feelings for him? Mayhap the babe was making her more emotional than usual?

Yes. The babe. That was why he was here, because they needed to discuss it. He would not wait another moment.

"Tell me, why did you go to such lengths to make yourself undesirable?" he murmured once her tears had dried. He thought he knew, but he wanted to hear it from her lips. It was time to force her to reveal what she was hiding from him.

"I could not bear the idea of..."

She stopped and her hand moved to her stomach as if she'd become accustomed to seeking comfort in the babe she was growing in her womb. At the last moment she bunched her fist and let her arm drop by her side. Cameron inhaled as his suspicions were confirmed. He had guessed that there would be more than wanting to ensure she did not appeal to men behind her desperate gesture. She had done this for their child. Rather than risk having the bairn hurt during an assault, she had cut herself.

His heart squeezed and melted at the same time because in this moment he knew for certain that not all hope was lost. She loved the bairn he had given her, in spite of everything, because she loved him.

"The idea of...?" he encouraged her softly.

Just when he thought she would find the courage to tell him, she straightened her spine and slid down from his lap, her face a blank mask once more.

"The idea of being taken against my will. Up until my arrival in Scotland, I had been in control of who I welcomed in my bed. It scared me to think that I might not be one day. McDonald thought he could force me to precipitate a union between us. The peddler thought he could rape me just because I was 'a beautiful woman' and he felt desire for me. I could not risk stirring another man's lust."

Aye, undoubtedly, her fear of rape would have weighed in the balance, but he knew that was not the main reason for hurting herself the way she had done. It would have been excruciatingly painful, and she would not have acted so decisively had she had only herself to protect.

"So you cut yourself, thinking it would be enough to keep men at bay?"

She swallowed. "I had intended to do more, but William stopped me. He walked in on me and was horrified."

"I bet he was." Cameron could not imagine the shock of finding her, a blade in hand, her face and neck covered in blood. Had it been him, he wasn't sure how he would have handled it. He would have to make sure to thank the man for stopping Bethan before she hurt herself any further. Really the list of what he owed Sir William was getting ridiculously long. "And so, to make sure you weren't assaulted by men who thought you defenseless, he offered to marry you?"

Her hesitation was brief, but unmistakable. "Yes."

Ah. So that was not the moment it had happened, then. Cameron guessed her friend would have asked a few weeks later, upon realizing she was with child and ruined. His chest tightened. He should have been there to rejoice in the news, share the moment with her, instead of letting her worry about the future of a babe who would be called a bastard if she remained unmarried.

Well, he would be there the next time she swelled with his child, and every time after that.

"Shall I tell you why I think you agreed to marry Sir William?" When she didn't answer, he took both her hands in his, locking his gaze with hers. This was it. She would not be allowed to deny she was with child a moment longer. "This is a mutually beneficial union. He saves you from unwanted attention and a ruined reputation and you provide him with the heir he would never have had otherwise."

"The... W-what do you mean?" she stammered.

"Ealasaid, I ken you are carrying my child," he said, finally placing a hand on her stomach. It was taut, just as he had guessed, and ever so slightly curved. His heart skipped a beat and then started to pound hard in his chest. "I ken that is why you were so desperate not to fall in the clutches of another man, why you sacrificed yourself, why it was imperative that you marry as soon as possible, why you accepted Sir William's offer. I will never thank him enough for the comfort and protection he offered you these last few months, but I will not let him do what I should be doing myself. There is another way to protect your reputation and ensure your protection. Marry me."

"You said I would be free to marry the man of my choice this time." Her eyes were filling with tears again.

"I am the man of your choice, me, and no other. And you are the only woman I will ever want."

"You don't want a wife," she reminded him weakly.

"I've changed my mind. I want this wife." He brought her hand to his lips to place a kiss on her ring finger. "This woman."

"You don't—"

He knew what she was about to say but he didn't let her

finish. "But I do. I want to marry you because I love you, not because you are now rich or because it is the right thing to do. I would want to marry you without the child you're about to give me. I took you against the wall because I could not stop myself a moment longer. I bedded you because I wanted you. I still do. I am prepared to wait if that's what you want, I'm prepared to woo you if that's what you need, I'm prepared to beg if that's what it takes. The only thing I won't do is give up. Do you imagine I would abandon my bairn or let anyone else take you away from me? I almost lost you to Dougal, Malcolm McDonald and God knows who else. I am not leaving this place without you so you might as well surrender now and spare us months of suffering."

"You truly love me?" She sounded both hopeful and wary, as if she feared believing him.

"Aye. *Tha gaol agam ort.* I cannot make it plainer than in my own language. Now you tell me you love me in Welsh so I know you mean it."

To his relief, she only hesitated for a heartbeat, then said, tears rolling down her cheeks. "*Rwy'n dy garu di.*"

"Thank you. You have no idea how much I needed to hear that."

She gave a shaky laugh, her mouth quivering. "You don't know what I said. I could have been asking you to get me a cup of mead, and you wouldn't know."

"Nay. That was no request for mead. I saw the truth of your words in your eyes."

"Cameron."

"No more tears." He wiped her cheek gently, then kissed her scar with reverence, running his tongue along its length, up, then down, before falling at her feet. "I would have cut off my right hand rather than seeing you hurt thus, especially considering you cut yourself to protect my bairn. But what is done is done. Promise me you will never hide your face again, from me or anyone. You are beautiful. Always will be."

His hand found its way to her stomach again and he smiled when he imagined his son in there, warm, and safe inside her body. Or was it one of the wee daughters he'd always wanted? His heart felt ready to burst at the idea of meeting the babe in a few months' time. He couldn't wait.

"Oh, my love. That I should be the one to give you a child... The one looking after you, the one lucky enough to marry you..." He shook his head, pressing his lips just above her navel. It was too much happiness for one man.

Bethan placed her hand on his cheek. "I haven't agreed to marry you yet, you know," she said softly.

"Nay. But you will."

She bit her bottom lip, doubt assailing her. "There is William to consider. After all he did, I don't want him to—"

He silenced her with a kiss on the palm still cradling his cheek. She was worried she would hurt her friend's feelings, and after all the man had done for her, he could understand. But Cameron knew she could accept his offer without scruples.

"Sir William gave me his blessing earlier. He will not stand in my way. The man's not a fool. He knows I'm the one you're meant to be with. So let's go and tell him the good news."

The following week passed in a blur.

With a wedding to organize, there was much to do. The days were spent sending invitations, choosing food for the banquet, getting the clothes ready. To everyone's surprise, Bethan's stomach had expanded almost overnight, and the gown she had selected for her wedding—to William, originally—had to be discarded in favor of one with a more forgiving cut.

The nights were spent in a flurry of passion that left Bethan breathless. Knowing William would not disapprove, and not caring about what everyone else thought, she and Cameron had not waited to be married to share a bed. Let people talk, they would not be hypocrites and sneak around to one another's rooms at night when everyone could see they had already anticipated their vows.

The morning that was to be their wedding day she was awakened by a ray of sunshine falling over her face. She smiled. It had rained the whole week, so she could not help but see this as a good omen. This union was blessed indeed. Not that she doubted it.

"*Madainn mhath,*" she murmured in Cameron's ear. It was always a good morning when she woke up next to him, nestled in his warmth.

"*Bore da* to you too," he rumbled back, eyes still closed. They had started to learn each other's language, as they had agreed their children would speak Gaelic and Welsh as well as English.

She gave him a slow, languorous kiss. By the time she drew away, his eyes were no longer closed, and every part of him was wide awake, most noticeably the one hidden under the sheet.

Perfect. That was just what she wanted. They still had some time before they started the day, and she would make the most of it. The wedding was not planned until later in the afternoon.

"Mm. I know that spark in your eye, Lady Campbell. You're up to mischief."

Bethan giggled. Cameron, after having insisted many times that she was not a lady, had taken to calling her Lady Campbell even though she had no right to the title yet.

"Not mischief, precisely." She pressed herself tighter against him and brought her hand to the bulge at his groin. "But there is something I'd like to try. You know I told you on the day we met that I had never pleasured anyone on my knees before?"

The gray in his eyes caught on fire. "I seem to remember something to that effect, aye. Imagining you at my feet got me all hard, though I had not seen you properly at the time. The dirt on your face could have covered all manners of sins, warts, hairy moles, and even scales, but there was something about you that drew me irresistibly. Then I saw you in Castell Esgyrn and I knew I would like nothing more than being pleasured by you."

"I know. You did tell me you imagined me welcoming you between my lips." She had not forgotten his scandalous words, nor the effect they'd had on her. She had gone hot all over. Just like now, hot all over—and slick in a very specific place.

"Och." Cameron groaned, as if he could not bear to be reminded of how crude he'd been that day. "Love, I'm sorry, I should never have told you this."

"Mayhap not at the time, but there is nothing wrong with you saying it now. And if you must know, I have thought about it often." The heat within her became unbearable as she made the confession. "I would like to start now. It's not fair that you should always be the one to give me pleasure."

"I love nothing more than to give you pleasure, *mo chridhe*," he interposed softly. "And seeing you come undone under my kisses."

"I know, I love it too and I'm sure I will love seeing you come undone under mine." With those words, she threw the covers to the floor in an impatient gesture, uncovering his naked body. A gasp escaped her lips at the sight she would never tire of. Was this man really hers and his magnificent body hers to do with what she wanted? Apparently so.

Her fingers closed around his shaft. His very hard, very eager shaft. This was not a new caress, but she had not dared do more yet. In any case, every time she'd thought she'd found the courage to finally put her lips on him, he'd distracted her by putting his on her and she had been too glad to let him lick her to dizzying heights of pleasure. But not today. Today she would do what they both wanted her to do.

"Do you still dream about me welcoming you between my 'full, sensual' lips? Do you still think I have the perfect mouth for sucking cock?" Why was it that saying the shocking words out loud caused heat to burst between her legs? Bethan had no idea, but it was delicious. She licked her lips suggestively, already sure of his answer.

"Bloody hell, yes, Ealasaid, I do. Your lips are pure perfection. *You're* pure perfection. Now. Take me in your mouth now," he rasped, arching his back in supplication. "Please. Show me how right I was to think you were made for this."

"Ah, but if you want me on my knees at your feet, you will have to stand up," she purred, giving him another stroke.

He moved with impressive speed and fluidity, taking her with him. "All right. I'm up," he said unnecessarily.

So she could see. Definitely up.

"Will you show me what you like?" she breathed, rubbing a cheek against his hip. She had a fair idea of what she was to do, but she wanted to make sure to please him.

"Whatever you choose to do I guarantee I will like," he grunted, pulling at her shift. Unlike him, she had always been too cold to sleep naked. With luck that would change in the spring, now that she was sharing a bed with a big, brooding man. "But please, hurry," he said, once he'd thrown her garment to the floor.

Smiling at the urgency in his voice, Bethan started to trail kisses all over his body, lingering over the places she loved the most. The smooth, rounded shoulders, the flat stomach, the soft hairs around his navel. She would never have credited it but the simple act of dropping to her knees in front of a man sent a burst of heat between her legs. Arousal spiked through her, before settling between her legs. She was going to enjoy this.

"Whatever I choose to do, you say?" she murmured, speaking against the warm skin of his thigh. The urge to bite it was overwhelming. She nipped at the skin, gently.

"Yes," he answered in a rasp. "Anything."

"How about this then?"

Cameron almost swallowed his tongue when the first lick over his sensitive skin sent shards of burning ice through the base of his spine. Then when Bethan wrapped her lips around the engorged head of his shaft, he lost the ability to breathe normally. Her mouth was scalding hot and so wet and soft, that he knew he would not last long.

Fascinated, he watched himself disappear between her full, sensual lips and remerge, wet and impossibly hard, before being swallowed up again. In and out, in and out, over and over again. Ah, he'd been right, she had the perfect mouth for this, and the perfect mind, bold and generous. Utterly lost to his pleasure, he fisted his hand into her hair to bring her closer to him. She glanced up at him, the connection between them adding yet another thrill to the moment. How many times had he dreamed of this? Hundreds. And yet, now that the moment had come, he wasn't sure he was going to be able to withstand it for much longer.

"Ealasaid," he warned, "anymore of this and I will spill into your mouth."

She hummed, an unmistakable invitation to do so. The minx! How had he not guessed she wouldn't be shocked by his warning? Could he accept her scandalous offer? No woman had ever agreed to do that for him yet and the temptation to let go was fierce. Still one last vestige of sanity prevailed. This was the first time she'd taken a man in her mouth, he should...

Cameron tried to wrench away but she didn't let him, grabbing the back of his thighs with surprisingly strong fingers. A series of Gaelic curses escaped his lips. If she wanted this, then so be it. A moment later he had no other choice but to surrender. The fingers in her hair tightened. A harsh growl escaped his throat, and he bucked his hips one last time, emptying all he had into her waiting mouth.

When he finally dared to look down, Bethan was looking at him from under her lashes, the look one of perfect innocence.

Dear God, how was it possible to love someone so much?

He collapsed onto the bed, utterly drained.

"Now you won't have to imagine me on my knees. You will be able to remember what it feels like instead," she purred, coming to straddle him.

"Aye. Though I might need to refresh my memory from time to time."

She smiled. "Anytime."

"I would like nothing more than to fuck you right now, but you will have to give me a moment," he said, glancing at his cock, lying in its nest of copper curls. It was not as limp as it could be, but still not hard enough for allowing him to plunge inside her sweetness the way they needed it. "Fortunately, I still have my mouth."

A whimper betrayed her readiness. She started to roll onto her back, ready to offer him the treasure he craved. He stopped her with both hands at her waist and took a moment to admire her. Sat astride him, with her lips swollen from sucking on him, her breasts bared, and her stomach gently curved with his child, she had never been more alluring.

"I love you."

She smiled. "I love you too."

"Now, my lady. It seems to me you that you quite liked being on your knees, so that's where you'll stay."

In one move, he lifted her off his lap, to bring her nearer the wall. At the same time, he slid down the bed. Aye, perfect. The backs of her thighs were now pressed against his shoulders and her sweet, feminine folds were hovering just above his face. He could see the proof that licking him had sent her wild with need and his mouth started to water at the idea of tasting the desire he had awoken in her. Pleasuring him pleased her as much as pleasuring her pleased him, it seemed. A growl escaped his throat. What had he done to deserve such a wild woman, such a wonderful wife?

"Yes," Bethan cried out when she understood what he had in mind. This was a new position, but something he had wanted to try for a while, and judging from the hoarseness in her voice, she was all too happy to indulge him.

"Hold on to the bed frame if you need to. I'm going to lick you until you come in my mouth and when you think you can't move, I'll have recovered enough to take you as hard and fast as I need." He was so aroused it wouldn't take his cock long to recover from its shattering release. "You won't have to do a thing. I'll lie you down on your stomach and—"

"Cameron, stop talking, damn you! Didn't you promise to lick me? Do it."

Ever the bold vixen, Bethan grabbed a fistful of his hair and lowered herself onto his waiting mouth. Well, that was one way of shutting him up, he supposed. He groaned when her scent hit him and then closed his eyes when her taste exploded on his tongue.

Cameron was in heaven, doing what he loved best, surrendering to his lover's will. He would make sure to send them both to the stars and back.

And then he would make her his wife at last.

Chapter Sixteen

Two weeks after their wedding, Bethan and Cameron rode in through the gate of Castell Esgyrn at sunset, taking everyone by surprise. On the way they had first stopped at Castell y Ddraig to inform her brother of the events of the last few months. It was more than time she told Siaspar what had happened to her since they had last seen one another. Caught in the whirlwind of events of the past three months, she had not found the time or the courage to write. It had seemed harsh to shower him with the distressing news of Dougal's death, of her near abductions, of her carrying a child who would never know its real father—and have nothing good to add to mitigate the news. Then when William had offered to marry her, she had elected to wait until they were wed before traveling to Wales and assure her brother in person that all was well, or at least as well as it could be under the circumstances.

Now she was able to do even better and tell him she had married the man of her dreams and was going to start her family in a place she loved.

William, who'd become fast friends with Cameron, had insisted on accompanying them. Having known the Hunter family nearly all his life, he wished to see their seat in Wales at last. This was as good an opportunity as any and they had been more than happy to have him travel with them.

The three of them reached her brother's castle one sunny morning, and found Siaspar in the bailey, talking to his friend Rhodri. Heart bursting with joy, Bethan dismounted and ran up to him.

"*Chwaer!*" The term of endearment that had burst out at the sight of her, the one she had feared never to hear again, died on his lips. Instead of drawing her into the embrace she had expected, Siaspar held her at arms' length, fury distorting his face. "Tell me who dared to do that to you."

For a moment, Bethan wondered what he was talking about. Who had done what? Then it hit her. Of course, the scar! How could she have forgotten how she looked now, and how it would appear to him? William never passed any comments and Cameron never looked at her any differently than he had in the summer, making her feel like the most beautiful woman in the world. Because of that, it was easy for her to imagine herself looking the way she had before she cut herself.

Except that she did not, and she had worried her brother.

"It's nothing," she soothed, berating herself for her lack of foresight. "I should—"

"It's not nothing! Did *he* hurt you thus?" he asked her, glaring at Cameron, who was standing by his horse, waiting patiently. Though he didn't understand Welsh yet, he would have guessed what her brother was saying. Still, as he had nothing to blame himself for, he appeared as calm as ever. "Or your damned Scottish husband? Is that him, by the black horse? He's a dead man if he—"

"No, this is not Dougal. I will explain about the scar in due time." It would not be an easy conversation, but she owed him the truth. It wasn't fair to allow him to place blame on Cameron or anyone else for something she had done herself. "But first let me introduce you to Sir William Parry, my friend from Sheridan Manor."

Siaspar nodded, marginally appeased. He had heard much about the man over the years, and knew how close the two of them were. "Welcome to Castell y Ddraig. It is good to finally meet you. My laird, welcome back."

"Thank you," the two men said in unison.

"But what are you doing here?" Siaspar asked next. "Is there—"

"If we can have a drink first, I promise to tell you all."

A moment later, around a table laden with delicacies, Bethan explained everything. There was no need to hide the truth, she was with the three men who loved her most in the world and they would not judge her. By the time she had finished, her brother was no longer glaring at Cameron, even if he was having difficulty suppressing his ire at the thought of all she'd had to endure.

"Welcome to the family," he said, raising his cup to him. "I will admit I am relieved to see Bethan never married the Scot."

"Well, I am a Scot, in case you hadn't noticed," her husband answered with a side smile—and a stronger than usual accent.

"You know what I mean."

"Aye. And I, too, am glad your sister didn't marry Dougal. He wasn't a bad man, but he would never have made her happy."

"There is one last thing to tell you," Bethan said, taking Cameron's hand to place it on her stomach. It was bigger than usual, but not so big that it was noticeable when she was sat down. In the bailey earlier, she had been wrapped up in her cloak and Siaspar's attention had been wholly focused on her scar. She was confident he wouldn't have noticed anything. "I'm with child."

Never had she been her brother speechless before. Eyes brimming with tears she took the hand he had held out to her across the table.

"*Llongyfarchiadau.*"

"Congratulations," she heard Cameron translate to William while she wiped a tear from her cheek.

They spent three wonderful days with Siaspar, hunting, feasting, riding, laughing together. Then finally they departed, with assurances to write regularly with news of his niece or nephew. Such was Bethan's impatience and the pace she set that it didn't take them long to reach Castell Esgyrn.

Gwenllian was the first to see her and ran into her arms.

"Bethan! I knew you would not forget us, even though you're now married to the Scot." She looked around the bailey and, seeing only Cameron and William, asked. "But what are you doing here, and where is your husband?"

"Here." Bethan reached out to Cameron, taking his hand in hers. "We got married last week," she added in English for his benefit.

"But that's not... I don't understand. That's not Dougal, that's the grizzled old uncle who came in the summer!"

A laugh escaped Bethan's throat. From the moment they had received the letter informing her of the arrival of the Scots, Gwenllian had taken to calling Laird Campbell, who'd been nothing more than a name at the time, "the grizzled old uncle."

"It is the uncle," she agreed. "But there's nothing old or grizzled about him."

The irony was not lost on her. Her father had wanted to marry her to the future Laird Campbell and restore family's prestige. Well, she had done both. She was a rich woman and a lady at the head of a powerful clan. But more importantly, she was a happy woman, and about to become a mother.

"Come. I sense this will be quite a tale to tell. We'll join the others so you can tell us all at the same time." Her friend sounded delighted, and not a little excited at the prospect. "Your timing couldn't have been better, as we were just about to eat."

As they entered the familiar hall illuminated by the light of a dozen candles, Gwenllian called out to the people assembled at the far end, away from the draughts trying to insinuate themselves through the door. The whole Hunter family was here. Lord and Lady Sheridan were sitting side by side, each with a huge wolfhound at their feet. Rhys was playing dice in a corner with his youngest sister Seren. Jane, her baby son Madoc on her lap, was sitting in front the hearth, while Griffin and their six-year-old twins tended to the fire. Opposite her, Siân, one hand on her swollen belly, was watching her husband Christopher, chase their three daughters around the table. It was a scene of perfect bliss, but she found herself imagining the hall of Nead an Diabhail instead, populated with the family she and Cameron would soon have.

"Guess who's just arrived?" Gwenllian asked everyone, before turning to face her. The joy in her eyes disappeared in the space of a heartbeat, replaced by a look of pure horror. "Dear God, what happened to you?"

Bethan cursed herself for not warning her friend in advance about the scar. Hadn't Siaspar's reaction the other day proved that people would be shocked upon seeing her? She should have remembered. "I will explain everything later. 'Tis nothing."

Lord Sheridan walked over to them, all fierce intent. "'Tis not nothing. Is your husband mistreating you, Bethan?" he asked, choosing Welsh to make sure to exclude Cameron. "Is that why you're here?"

"My husband is the best man I've ever met. Let me introduce you to him," she answered, reverting back to English as she took Cameron's hand in hers. "But you already know Laird Campbell, don't you?"

A stunned silence filled the room. For a moment all eyes were on her. Then the baby on Jane's lap started to giggle uncontrollably when one of the dogs licked his hand. Just like that, the tension broke, and Lady Sheridan walked over to her, her face wreathed in smiles.

"Come. You must all be exhausted and hungry," she said, ever the peacemaker. "We were about to eat, you'll be pleased to hear."

"Thank you."

Everyone joined them around the table, greeting William, who was delighted to see people he hadn't seen in a long time. Bethan had never felt happier. Before they sat down, Cameron removed her cloak, the gesture bringing attention to her stomach.

It was Seren's turn to gasp. "You're with child!"

Bethan's lips stretched into a smile when all eyes fell on her. Trust the girl to notice it straight away.

"I am." Indeed, though she looked nothing like Siân, who was approaching her term, her own stomach would be hard to miss. The dress she was wearing was tighter than the one she had worn at Castell y Ddraig.

"Oh, it seems like there is much to tell indeed!" Gwenllian cried out as servants placed the first dishes on the table.

"There is. So let me start at the beginning."

That night, in bed, Bethan nestled herself against her husband. The welcome they'd received had been everything she could have wished for. It had been a good idea to come in person and see the joy on their faces when she told them her happy news. This time, when she left in a few days' time, the Hunter family would not worry about her. They would know she was going exactly where she wanted to go, with the Scot she had chosen for herself rather than the one who had been forced onto her.

"That has been one of the best evenings of my life, but now I'm exhausted," she said in a yawn.

"Do you..."

Cameron paused. He sounded unusually hesitant and, forgetting her fatigue a moment, Bethan lifted herself onto one elbow to look at him. "What is it?" Had she missed something tonight? It had seemed to her he was getting on well with every-one. Was she mistaken?

"Are you sure you want to come live in Scotland, *mo chridhe*? You seem so happy here."

She smiled, loving him for this question which must have cost him. What if she told him she didn't want to leave Wales? He was laird, he could not leave his clan, even supposing he'd wanted to settle in Wales. And yet he was giving her the option of remaining in her country. But she would not take it.

"I am happy here. But it's never really been my home. I want to build my home, with you in Nead an Diabhail, not here in Castell Esgyrn. I'm not a young girl anymore, forced to accept friends' charity but a married woman of some means, and about to become a mother. I want my own place. Scotland is just perfect for that." She landed a hand on her husband's muscular chest and started to stroke it with sensual gestures. "Besides, there is something in Nead an Diabhail that I hold very dear, something I would miss too much if I came back to live in Wales, something delicious to eat."

The growl in her ear sent shivers down her spine. "Stop talking and touching me thus, wife, or I'll feed that delicious thing to you now, exhausted or not."

She looked at him, careful to appear full of hope. "Oh, you mean you've brought oats all the way here? Why didn't you tell me before?"

"Oats?" The look of bewilderment on her husband's face was priceless. "What the devil are you talking about?"

"Why, porridge, of course, which is utterly delicious, and has become one of my favorite things to eat to break my fast," she answered innocently. "What are *you* talking about?"

Cameron flopped back down onto the bed with a groan. "Minx. You'll be the death of me."

Bethan took pity on him. "I'm tired now, but I swear, tomorrow morning, you can feed me anything you want, as long as it's Scottish." Her fingers closed around his shaft, which was already half-hard.

"Aye, well, every inch of me is as Scottish as it comes."

"Excellent. I can't wait."

"My laird. Welcome back."

"I thank you. Though I am not alone," Cameron said calmly, removing his gloves. "I have brought my wife with me. Please welcome Lady Campbell."

"*Wife?*"

"You're married?

Bethan couldn't help a smile at the incredulity in the men's voices. During the ride back home, she and Cameron had decided on the best way to tell the clan about their laird's recent wedding and had concluded that surprise would be the best option. He had taught her the Gaelic she needed to understand what he would tell the men upon arrival so that she would know when to step out of the shadows.

She did as arranged, keeping the right side of her face hidden by the hood of her cloak. She had learned her lesson the hard way in Wales, and knew she needed to warn the people who knew her before revealing her face.

When they recognized her for Dougal's former betrothed, the men stared, struck speechless. Angus took a step back, and

Hamish's eyes were in danger of bugging out of his face. Alone, Murdo didn't appear shocked. His mouth set in a smirk, he said something to Cameron in Gaelic, unaware that after two months of intense tutelage, she now had a passing understanding of the language. *Why am I not surprised?* she thought he'd said. She reddened. Had he known about her and Cameron? Apparently so.

In any case, even if he had not suspected anything in the summer, he would be forced to see that this wedding had not been a whim when he saw her stomach. She was now entering her last term, which explained the leisurely pace they had traveled from Wales, and it showed. Or at least it would when she removed her heavy fur cloak.

"My lady!" Angus exclaimed. She couldn't help a smile. Finally, he had every right to call her that. "You really married the laird?"

"I certainly did."

"Lucky bugger," she heard Murdo mutter between his teeth. The fact that he'd spoken loud enough for her to hear—and in English—indicated that he'd intended for her to understand what he'd said. She couldn't help a smile. Despite an unpromising start, she had come to like the gruff man, who was loyal and honest to a fault.

"Aye. I'm a very lucky bugger," Cameron said, drawing her to his side and placing a hand on her stomach. The evocative gesture exposed its rounded shape to all present. "And soon to be twice as lucky."

The hall erupted in congratulations and well wishes. No one seemed to mind that this babe had obviously been conceived before the wedding vows had been spoken. This homecoming was perfect, just what she had wished for.

"And Bethan now has a scar on her face," Cameron carried on. Such a matter-of-fact declaration. He could just as well have said: she now owns a second red gown. Bethan's insides melted in tenderness. How she loved this man, who always knew how to put her at ease. "Should anyone make her feel uncomfortable about it, they will soon find themselves sporting the same one on both cheeks, courtesy of my sword. Am I clear?"

"Aye!"

Thinking it best to get this over with, she removed the hood of her cloak and almost burst out laughing when no one so much as blinked. Cameron's fierceness had its advantages, it seemed.

While everyone went back to their tasks, she drew Angus and Murdo to one side, oddly intimidated. There was something she needed to tell them.

"I wanted to thank you for what you did for me the day Malcolm McDonald wanted to abduct me."

"Aye, well, as to that, we didn't do anything, and you ken it very well." Murdo kicked an invisible stone out of the way, his dismay obvious.

"You did precisely what we agreed, acting as decoys, placing yourselves in danger, escorting the fake Bethan out of Nead an Diabhail and allowing Cameron and me to slip away unnoticed. There was no need to do more. Getting killed would have achieved nothing, Morag would still have been abducted in my stead. Besides, you saw what happened." She reddened as indeed, they would have seen even more than her, who had left before the couple started rutting in earnest.

More kicking at stones that weren't anywhere to be seen. "Aye, we did, though we tried not to look."

"Have you any news of her?" Bethan had worried about the woman over the last few months. How had Malcolm McDonald taken the humiliation inflicted on him? Bold and deceitful as she had been, Morag had saved her and she would be loath to hear she had been harmed, or worse.

The two men exchanged an amused look that instantly set her mind at rest.

"She's about to give the man a child," Angus said. "From what we hear, he cannot get his hands off her. Don't worry about the lass. She took a gamble, and it seems it paid off."

Well. It would seem that both of them had won the man of their dreams in the end. Bethan relaxed.

"And speaking of which, my lady, I'm sure your husband already told you, but when Angus and I made it back to Nead an Diabhail after Morag's abduction, we found out it had been McBain allowing Donald McDonald into Crois Dhubh that night."

Bethan nodded. Indeed, Cameron had told her how his two loyal men had unearthed the traitor who had let the McDonalds in the night of the attack. He had also told her that Dougal's friend had recognized her for the woman outside the tavern during their ride to Scotland and had convinced himself she was really a whore and deserved nothing more than to be treated like one, away from his clan. At the time she had congratulated herself on the fact that Cameron had not been the one dealing with McBain, as she was sure that the traitor's punishment would have been exemplary, but when Murdo spoke, she saw that her relief might have been premature.

"The fool tried to tell everyone that you were a w—begging your pardon, a woman of ill repute. As if anyone in their right mind would believe such a thing. You'll be pleased to know that I dealt with him," he told her, crossing his arms over his chest. "He won't pose any threat to you ever again."

Since she wasn't sure she would like to hear what he had done, she didn't ask for any more details. That chapter of her life was closed.

That evening Bethan and Cameron stood at the top of the northern tower, the one overlooking the tranquil *loch*. In the moonlight, the surface was as smooth and shiny as a pool of quicksilver, the same shade as her husband's eyes. All around the hills, as dark and fluffy as pillows, created the perfect...well, nest for it. It was a breathtaking view, and she couldn't wait to come back in the morning to see it bathed in sunshine—or wrapped in mysterious fog, or drenched in rain, or blanketed with snow. It didn't matter which. Now that she was mistress of the place, she would get to see it every season.

She sighed. "I remember thinking this summer that I could imagine myself living here. I'm so glad I now have the chance to."

"I'm glad too, my love."

"In the end, Nead an Diabhail didn't live up to its fearsome name. I cannot imagine a more peaceful place, or one where I'd rather be."

Cameron was holding her tight with her back against his chest as protection against the bitter wind, both his hands cradling her stomach in a familiar gesture. "Do you think we'll have a laddie or a wee lassie?" he whispered in her ear.

Bethan placed her hands over his. She'd been wondering the same thing, though she didn't mind either way. Besides, she intended to have many more children, so chances were, she would get both sons and daughters. "I think it might be a boy this time, but I don't know why."

"I think the same, and I don't ken why either. Perhaps because, as I told you, my family seems to favor boys." He landed a kiss on her hair. "Whichever way, it will be the loveliest bairn anyone has ever seen."

Epilogue

"Little Callum is such a beautiful child."

"He is."

Bethan beamed at William, who looked slightly at a loss now that her son had woken up and held out her hands. Relieved, her friend handed her the baby back and sat down in the chair opposite her. He had been here for a week, having come for a visit as soon as he had heard about the birth of his godson. His presence had been all the more appreciated as Cameron had gone to visit the neighboring clan and she was missing him dreadfully.

"But then I suppose it is no wonder he should be a beauty, considering how good his father looks."

"Thank you!" Bethan gave a tinkling laugh and placed a kiss on the baby's soft hair. Indeed, her son was, as predicted, "the loveliest bairn anyone has ever seen"—and a boy. No matter, she meant to try until she gave her husband the daughters he was dreaming of. Not that either of them had complained at being handed a son when Callum had been born. "I know where I stand. Callum's beauty is to be wholly attributed to Cameron. I will not—"

"Who dares utter such nonsense?" a husky voice interrupted, coming from the doorway.

Her heart skipped a beat, as it did every time she set eyes on her husband. She could tell from his disheveled hair that he had rushed back to reach Nead an Diabhail—and his family—before dark.

"Cameron! You're back!"

He walked in and placed a kiss on her temple before giving little Callum a caress on the cheek. The child was now a month old, his parents' pride and joy.

"My son is indeed beautiful, but it has nothing to do with me. He's the image of my wife, and any fool can see it."

"Are you calling me a fool?" William asked with mock outrage.

"What if I were? Will you take issue with it?"

"I dare not. Your skill with the sword far exceeds mine."

A laugh. "It does. That's what experience does for you, pup. Though you have nothing to fear from me. I would never attempt anything against my wife's dearest friend, as well you know," he added with a smile.

"Indeed I do. I have your eternal gratitude." William was model of resignation.

"How about I prove it to you by suggesting that my squire help you improve your footwork while you're in Scotland? I taught him myself and he's very good. He should be able to show you what you need. In turn, you could help with his English which, at the moment, is only very basic. I know he would like to visit England some time."

"Alasdair, you mean?" Bethan enquired, suddenly understanding what her husband was trying to do. "The one everyone says looks just like you?"

"Aye. I have lost count of how many times I've been asked if he is not my bastard half-brother." There was a mischievous glint in her husband's eye she knew only too well. "Indeed, he is similar to me in almost every way."

"*Almost* every way?" William stood up, hope making his voice hoarse.

"Aye, as he seems to have no interest in marrying and producing bairns. I wonder why that might be."

"I can think of a few very valid reasons. Well, I suppose it is time I started improving my footwork, so I'd better go find him."

William took his leave without another word, leaving Cameron and Bethan to laugh at the success of their little scheme. Would that her friend finally found the man for him, like she had found the one for her...

"How is my son? I've missed him, you know," Cameron said, coming to kneel at her feet. She handed him the babe, who fit perfectly in the crook of his arm. The bond between father and son had been strong from the start.

"He's happy and content. Growing stronger by the day."

"Good. How about his mother? I've missed her too."

"Now, *she* has been pining after her husband and growing more impatient by the day. He's been gone for far too long."

He smiled. "It's been four days, Ealasaid."

She smiled back. "As I said. Far too long. William is good company during the day but he's useless at night. Only one person can give me what I need."

"Aye?" The gray eyes flashed. "And who is that, I wonder?"

Bethan kissed him as passionately as she was able. "You. My Scot."

About the Author

As far back as I remember, I have been attracted to the Middle Ages, to knights in shining armour and their ladies in spectacular dresses. Now I get to write about them, I feel like the luckiest woman in the world. Being French and married to a Brit makes each book I write extra special, as our countries share a long and sometimes painful past. But in the end, in life as well as in fiction, love conquers all!

I have published several medieval romances under my own name, including series, and also have a pen name, Judith Falcon, for spicier projects, still in historical romance.

Join my newsletter and check out my other books on virginiemarconato.com.

Also by Virginie Marconato

The Welsh Rebels

A Husband for Esyllt

A Savior for Branwen

A Second Chance for Carys

A Rogue for Siân

A Lover for Lady Jane

A Scot for Bethan

The Noble Norsemen

Taming the Wolf

Soothing the Beast

Wooing the Devil

Baiting the Bear

Tempting the Saxon

Seducing the Warrior

Loving the Blacksmith